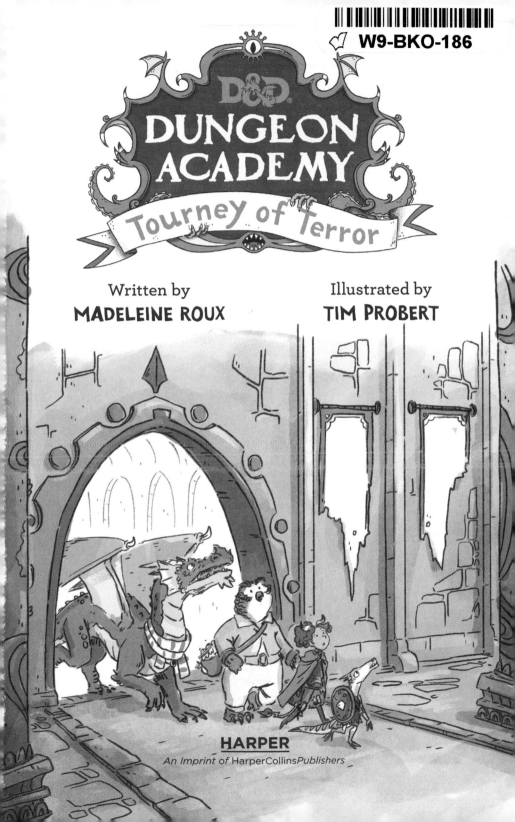

D&D

DUNGEON ACADEMY

Tourney of Terror

Written by
MADELEINE ROUX

Illustrated by
TIM PROBERT

HARPER
An Imprint of HarperCollinsPublishers

Snabla, the Courageous Kobold

Bauble, the Know-it-All

1

Zellidora "Zelli" Stormclash shielded her eyes from the blowing sand with her forearm, squinting against the harsh sunlight glinting off the dunes. Endless dunes. The desert seemed to go on forever, a demoralizing vastness of nothing. At her side, her faithful companions (and members of the Danger Club) Bauble the mimic, Hugo the owlbear, and Snabla the kobold pressed on, though Snabla stumbled and fell behind.

"Too hot," the kobold groused. He lifted his shield, hiding behind it as another gust of hot, arid wind cut against them like a gritty scimitar. "Cannot take . . . another ssstep."

Flash, the blink dog who kept them company, popped her head out of Hugo's bag and gave a hopeless howl.

Zelli reached for Snabla, taking hold of one skinny,

leathery arm before yanking him forward.

"It's here," she told him. "I just know it is."

Close, the wind seemed to whisper. *So close.*

"What's here?" Bauble asked. The mimic, who was traveling as a parasol in Hugo's grasp, coughed on a mouthful of grit carried on the gale.

Zelli suddenly went still. What was she searching for? Why couldn't she remember? She closed her eyes tightly and tried to picture . . . picture . . .

The dunes beneath their feet started to rumble. The Danger Club retreated a few steps, all of them struck silent and awed as the sand bounced and thrashed in higher and higher sprays, like marbles dancing on the skin of a tight drum. Beneath the sands, two massive stone slabs became visible, a split running between them. The gap widened, the stones parting, puffs of black particles rising from the cavernous void the slabs had guarded. *Smoke?* Zelli thought, but the particles were denser, almost like burnt snowflakes, if such a thing were possible. Splashes like the inverse of stardust, so dark they might have been fragments of night.

A voice spoke to her, as sinister and strange as the puffs of nightdust spraying from the tomb beneath the dunes. *The Lord of Death will rise. The great master awakens beneath forgotten sands. Death comes when the barrier is broken.*

"We shouldn't be here," Zelli blurted out. In her hand, Snabla's little arm felt as brittle as a wintry branch. She turned to him, and watched his eyes bug wide before he crumbled to dust.

"But you brought us here," Hugo told her, before he, too, was gone, blown away on a gust of hot desert wind.

You belong here.

Zelli finally recognized the voice. A dream! This was just a dream! She felt the ground tremble again, then woke up, realizing the rumbling was her bedframe as she jolted upright, tossing the blankets off in a flurry of hands and feet. She breathed hard, back in the warm, close familiarity of her housing at Dungeon Academy. Across the chamber, her ooze roommate, Bloppy, snored and burbled peacefully. Zelli scrubbed at her face with both hands, exhausted. It was the same nightmare she had suffered for three nights now—mindlessly wandering through the desert until at last she stumbled on a secret she was meant to find.

The times before, no voice had spoken to her. Now she knew who was responsible for her nightmares.

"Lord Carrion," she murmured, swinging her legs out of the bed and sighing. It had been months since she and the other members of the Danger Club had

gone toe to toe with the necromancer outside Horntree Village and defeated him. Defeated him, yes, but not before he had managed to threaten worse dangers and abduct dozens of villagers, as well as a handful of Dungeon Academy students. Those students had been the academy's finest: truly menacing, terrorizing monsters, and not just your average goblin swinging a rusty sword in a cave. For everyone else, life had gradually returned to normal—Bauble continued gleefully and vocally knowing everything; Hugo took up a crusade to form a community garden for the school; Snabla "borrowed" Bauble's homework and put all his energy into Hacking and Slashing class, squeaking by in every other subject. And Flash did what she did best: appearing and disappearing with a loud *pop* to the delight of her friends, leaving trinkets or bone crumbs in the bottom of Hugo's backpack.

When it was all said and done, Lord Carrion wound up bound and embarrassed, but ultimately his life was spared, and he was locked up deep beneath Dungeon Academy. The dean had insisted on taking him captive, and wherever he lurked in the school, he was busy sending Zelli terrifying visions.

"I know it's you," Zelli said, watching as the purplish light outside their window shifted, turning a lighter shade of bruised. "Now I just have to do something about it."

Zelli shrugged out of her linen nightshirt and into a pair of brown trousers and a purple tunic. She grabbed her belt and wooden sword, and buckled on her leather armor, then quietly left her warm, waiting bed behind. Defeating the necromancer had not made Zelli overconfident. Before hefting her bag onto her shoulders, she checked to make sure the special little jar at the bottom was there and, more important, tightly sealed.

A few monster students wandered sleepily through the halls as she went by dawn's light to the big, creaking lift that would take her down to the academic levels of the school for monsters. She was pretty sure the bugbear she passed was sleepwalking while muttering about buttered toad legs. *At least someone is having pleasant dreams*, she thought.

It occurred to her that Bauble and Hugo would have sage advice on what to do about her nightmares, but this felt like a problem that couldn't go on probleming. She needed answers, and one gross, evil necromancer had them. Of course, Dean Zxaticus and the other professors had not felt the need to inform her or any other students where they were holding Lord Carrion, but Zelli had a hunch: mysteriously, the usual detention hall had been off-limits to students, punishments

instead carried out in the spare dungeon next to Professor Gast's classroom. Well, it was also a dungeon, but learning *did* happen there, if one could survive the droning, interminable lectures.

Zelli traversed the darkened halls of the academy quickly and quietly, avoiding the traps, wary of startling the clouds of bats waiting in the eaves to descend with their boisterous flapping and shrieking. When she arrived at the former detention location, the Hall of Eternal Suffering & Monotony, she found it guarded by a single sleeping cyclops. Durg, usually a groundskeeper, slumbered beside the ominously tall, iron-barred door with her legs straight out in front of her, a healthy string of drool the width of a goblin's wrist dripping from mouth to shoulder. Her snores vibrated the uneven cobbles beneath Zelli's boots.

Glancing up and down the empty corridor, Zelli tiptoed close to Durg and gave a gentle nudge with her elbow. The cyclops slept on, not even a hitch in her tremendous breath. Holding a breath of her own, Zelli slowly turned the rusting metal handle on the door, slid it open, and stuffed herself inside the gap. As the door slid shut again, she heard Durg snort and startle, make a noise of confusion, then settle back down again.

Zelli didn't need a torch of her own to safely navigate the hall, for hot, bright lava churned far below

the bridge and suspended platform that made up the chamber. She hurried across the bridge, her skin prickling with fear. As Zelli neared the platform at the other end of the rickety bridge, the young warrior noticed all the desks and the podium had been removed. A single form lay crumpled on the stone, bound there by thick, heavy chains and manacles.

Lord Carrion, once proud, cruel, and stubborn, had withered somewhat, his cheeks even more sunken and skull-like now. His embroidered purple robe was tattered and stained, but when he heard her tread and saw her, his eyes were still glinting, alarmingly vigilant and ever-mean.

"You got my message." He chuckled. The laugh sent a sharp chill down Zelli's spine. She *hated* that laugh.

"Listen up, bogbreath. I know you're the one sending me nightmares. Cut it out."

Lord Carrion showed his teeth. "Such hostility. I thought you were an adventurer. Like your mother?"

Zelli grabbed the hilt of her sword. "I'm not here to discuss my mother."

"What does she think about your ridiculous little costume, I wonder. . . ."

"Leave me alone!" Zelli almost shouted, then remembered she was meant to be sneaking. As a habit, she reached out to check the horns on her head, making sure they were present and not crooked. Humans, quite understandably, were hated by monsters and forbidden from entering the school. Masquerading as a minotaur at a learning institution for monsters was not exactly easy, but so far only her closest friends knew her secret. Lord Carrion had done battle against both Zelli and her birth mother, a famous human adventurer named Allidora Steelstrike.

Zelli chose to stay with her adoptive minotaur mothers. Which was none of Lord Carrion's stupid business.

"No more nightmares," she hissed. "I'm warning you, I'll tell Nihildris the mind flayer what you're up to and she'll make your head emptier than a dwarf's mead mug."

Lord Carrion lifted his head, which seemed to take a significant amount of effort. His hood fell back, revealing a spotted, bluish-pink scalp scarred by runic red markings. With obvious pleasure, he grinned. "Empty as . . . a desert, would you say?"

Zelli's eyes flared wider.

"So you saw it," Lord Carrion murmured. She didn't like his voice. He sounded oddly happy. Elated. "Yes. *Yes*, you have seen where she lies, the Lord of Death,

the Herald of Teeth and Eyes. Her coming presages the quieting of all the world. Her arrival is inexorable, but you can hasten it along, girl."

Zelli crossed her arms over her chest. "Whatever you tell me I'll just use against you."

"Your mind will change, girl, when you realize this annihilation cannot be stopped. It comes for your pathetic little academy, for your pathetic realm. You will fall on your knees and beg to be named her prophet, as I have, as we all will!" Lord Carrion shuddered and fell silent.

"But you said she's not here yet, this Lord of Death."

"Not yet," he admitted. "Close. Here now, and so close." His dark, vicious eyes rolled and then deliberately stared downward, as if pointing to something deep below the lava pit.

"*Here* here?" Zelli whispered. "What are you talking about?"

"Oh, the Star Mounts hold many secrets. Akhellon Ridge was not always a school. Its mysteries and magics run deep, deep as roots into Faerûn itself, fool child."

Akhellon Ridge. Zelli had no idea what he meant, but Bauble might, or their librarian. Whatever trap he was setting for her, Zelli refused to step into it. Her curiosity could be sated later, but she had come with one goal in mind. She reached into her backpack,

palming the sealed jar she had placed there while Lord Carrion giggled like a lunatic and stared at the ground.

Zelli marched closer to him, setting her jaw. "I mean it, Lord Carrion, no more nightmares. You will leave me alone or else."

His eyes flew back to hers, burning. "Or else? Ha. Or else what?"

With a flick of her wrist, Zelli unsealed the cloth on the jar and flung the contents at Lord Carrion, then leapt safely away.

"Or this!"

A fine rain of Lurkwood tickling spiders fell on the necromancer, skittering down into his purple robes as he grimaced and pulled on the chains that held him.

"I wouldn't want to be you for the next three days," Zelli snorted, satisfied. She turned and hurried back across the bridge, just as the tickling spiders found their mark and Lord Carrion began, hideously, to laugh.

2

Skeletons. *Skeletons.* This was what she got for listening to a crummy necromancer. It always had to be *something. Why never a peaceful jaunt into a cold, dark place to poke around?* Zelli wondered. *Why can't shadowy pits be filled with bouncing baby flumphs and feast-laden tables?*

Hours after her encounter with Lord Carrion, Zelli Stormclash was living up to her name: storming through the cavernous dark, torch held high, sweat dripping down her face as she heard the clickity-clack of angry skeleton feet fade. Hopefully the horrid mess of refuse littering the floor would trip up those delicate bony toes. Her boots were made for trudging, and so she trudged right around a wide stone pillar, shoved the book she had been carrying into her pack, and reached for her trusty wooden practice sword.

For a moment there was silence. She didn't dare breathe. Had they lost her? But then of course they couldn't miss the torch. . . . Could they see without eyeballs? Zelli scrunched up her face and shook her head. Too many questions!

Perhaps, and genuinely this time, it ought to be her last solitary outing when that outing could be considered an adventure. Hadn't she learned recently that it was good—even better—to rely on the aid of friends? She dragged in a steadying breath and told herself she wasn't afraid of the dark, or the unknown, or any of the many deep shadows surrounding her as she shivered behind a pillar in the lowest pit of the academy. And the lowest pit was truly saying something. She had traveled down from the regular dungeons—at least eight flights of spiraling stairs above—feeling the temperature drop and drop, ever more wisps of cobwebs brushing her face as she made her descent.

Zelli lofted her ever-burning torch higher, the only talisman against the encroaching dark. Well, that and her unshakable curiosity.

It didn't surprise Zelli that a school for monsters contained endless subterranean chambers full of

dangers and mysteries, but she had come after one dangerous mystery in particular—the secret Lord Carrion had mentioned. Akhellon Ridge. That was the only solid clue he had given. After speaking with Lord Carrion and, well, dousing him in spiders, she had gone directly to the library. The bespectacled, winged librarian, Shinka Bookbinder, was there dutifully organizing tomes behind the desk, present if a bit sleepy. It didn't take the old kobold long to find a book on Zelli's chosen topic, and Bookbinder returned from the history section in a cloud of dust, handing over a weighty, musty tome entitled *The Excavation of Akhellon Ridge.* Curled up on a bench in a slice of sunshine pouring in through the high, grime-encrusted library windows, Zelli sped her way through the book, hungry for secrets. She did not expect to discover that the mountain housing the Dungeon Academy had a history that wove back through time like a sinuous thread, and that the mountain had played host to a rotating cast of odd creatures and wanderers until it was finally hollowed out for the school grounds.

It held far more than the dark, gloomy classrooms she was so familiar with it, more than the dungeons and the detention lava pit, and more than the labyrinth students used to practice their lurking. Just as Lord Carrion had claimed, it was full of secrets.

Its original inhabitant, and eventual namesake, was a blue dragon from the Endless Wastes called Akhellon. After she vacated the mountain, a clan of kobolds moved in, and when they cleared off, a near-forgotten order of wizards and necromancers arrived thereafter. All these comers and goers apparently took up residence in the natural cave system of the mountain, a cave system that was expanded upon greatly to create what Zelli and her friends knew today as Dungeon Academy. On page 943, Zelli stumbled across the prize:

> For centuries, adventurers and treasure
> seekers sought to explore the deepest recesses
> of Akhellon Ridge. Eventually, the flow of
> delvers slowed to a trickle and then ceased
> altogether, for what begins as fact soon
> becomes legend, which passes into rumor, and
> finally fades to a whisper. Some historians
> claim the adventurers hunted a perfect
> sapphire the size of a dragon's egg; others tell
> of a powerful keystone, the Nexus Marker,
> which was said to have powered the mountain's
> magical barrier.

Beside the excerpt, the author had helpfully illustrated a subterranean passage in the mountain, a tall cavern with tumbled rocks and fallen adventurers, though one hopeful seeker stood, torch held high, showing an odd pattern decorating the rock wall. Zelli doubted very much that a necromancer like Lord Carrion was interested in a shiny gem. A powerful key, however, might be far more tempting. She didn't exactly understand the ins and outs of what a Nexus Marker might be, but she knew that between her and the other members of the Danger Club, they could likely find an answer. More presently, she felt certain she could heft her own torch and find that same design depicted in the book.

"It has to be here somewhere," Zelli sighed, working her way along the curved stone wall of the pit. Her boots scattered pebbles, brittle old bones, and the scraping claws of what she hoped were not intellect devourers. Those were nasty—crusty little brains running around on clawed feet, ready to feed on the intelligence of any thinking creature. Zelli shivered. Running her hand along the wall, she found it naturally cool to the touch and a little damp. Just like a cave. She then imagined thousands of years of ghosts wandering along beside her—kobolds, necromancers, and even a dragon. It gave her a shiver. A feathery wisp of cobweb danced across her forehead, making her leap back, screeching and swinging her torch.

The uneven glow of the torch illuminated the cavern above, and the remains of what seemed to her like an entire city of spiderweb bridges crisscrossing and weaving together, funnel-like, disappearing up into the higher reaches of the pit. She then remembered the awful spiders that infested the cave where the Danger Club defeated the necromancer—the sound of those chittering critters haunted her as regularly as Lord Carrion's wild laugh. It didn't help that Bauble, after hearing about Zelli's nightmares, had supplied the fact that one was never more than a few arm's lengths away from a creepy-crawly.

Zelli shuddered again and took a deep breath. Darkness, creepy-crawlies, the memories of long-past inhabitants . . . She wouldn't let it deter her. She was part of the Danger Club, and they had faced down insurmountable odds. But that had been together, and now she was alone.

She heard a soft, long scratch to her right along the floor, a bony hand wrapping around the edge of the pillar. *Out of time.* Zelli spun and lashed out with her training sword, the wood slashing through the

skeleton's rib cage, sending bones flying. But that was just one of many. *Too* many. She backed up toward the stairs leading out of the pit, deciding it would be better to survive the onslaught and explain it all to a teacher than perish there in that disgusting, dark hole.

Her shoulder bumped something hard and cold, and she whirled around again, colliding with another reanimated pile of bones. *Blast it all,* she thought. They had her surrounded! Her heart sank, realizing she was way too far below the surface to call for help. Even in the total darkness, she could feel the skeletons closing in . . . a tightening, inexorable circle . . .

Until the one she had bumped into on her way to the stairs suddenly and without warning exploded. She ducked, gasping, whirling to face the shower of bone shards in time to find two bright torches bobbing toward her. As soon as the expanding, welcome pool of light reached her, she let out a laughing breath—there was Flash, the blink dog, hovering in midair after breaking the skeleton like a dry pile of twigs. A furry, feathered face appeared above the pup. Hugo!

"Watch out!" the owlbear called, pointing at an advancing foe.

"Thisss one isss mine!" Snabla, the kobold, danced forward, nimble on his scaly little legs, and bashed the skeleton with the broad side of his beloved shield. Jabbing with his torch, he managed to catch the tattered

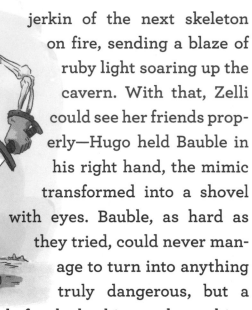

jerkin of the next skeleton on fire, sending a blaze of ruby light soaring up the cavern. With that, Zelli could see her friends properly—Hugo held Bauble in his right hand, the mimic transformed into a shovel with eyes. Bauble, as hard as they tried, could never manage to turn into anything truly dangerous, but a shovel would do nicely for the bashing and smashing of dry, crumbly things.

"All together!" Bauble cried, a jagged little mouth forming across the flat of the shovel.

Zelli didn't need any more encouragement—she turned and leapt back toward the skeletons, watching as ones on fire pinwheeled through the horde, lighting up the others as they went. Flames blazing, Zelli watched as Flash teleported into the rib cage of another skeleton and popped it apart with a joyous yip and a floppy, flailing tongue. With only a dozen or so skeletons left, the Danger Club easily dispatched them, and with each collapsed pile of knuckles and femurs and toes, Zelli felt a rush of relief.

And gratitude.

Pop—Smash—Bash—C-Crack!

When all the skeletons had been dispatched, Hugo hurried over to the last smoking, smoldering pile of bones and stamped out the dwindling fire. The torchlight dyed his silvery-white feathers orange as he blinked down at her in obvious confusion.

"What are you doing down here alone, Zelli?" he asked. "We couldn't find you anywhere. . . ."

"Come and look," she said, leading them back toward the odd engraving she had found. "But don't touch anything!"

"Sssnabla wouldn't want to," the kobold lisped, kicking aside a few scattered rib bones. Flash disappeared for an instant, reappearing on Hugo's shoulder. "Everything down here ssstinks!"

When they stood before the correct spot, Zelli took Hugo's torch, holding it out toward the wall. This was where she had noticed a few grooves in the uneven, slick surface. Reaching forward, she followed the indentations, tracing them with her palm, curving up toward dulled and dusty gemstones placed at intervals along the design. Zelli took a step back again, taking in the whole picture—it was just like the image in the book she had found. Here was the door-like design on the cave wall.

"What is it?" Bauble gasped. Hugo helpfully tilted shovel Bauble forward for a better look.

Fear settled over Zelli like an icy mantle. . . . The design reminded her so much of the runes on Lord Carrion's robes, and the purple gemstones were just the same color of the odd substance he had used to beguile the students and villagers. These gemstones, however, were dim with neglect, covered in a thick layer of grime.

Hugo stretched out his hand, as if to wipe the dust off one of the gems.

"No!" she cried, grabbing his feathered wrist. "We don't know where the door leads or what it might do!"

"Oh dear," Hugo gasped, snatching his hand back.

"How did you find this?" asked Bauble, eyes wide as they studied the odd door-like etching.

"I might have paid Lord Carrion a quick visit," Zelli explained, brushing a bit of powdered bone off her tunic.

Hugo rushed forward, taking her by the arm. "Alone?"

"I had to!" She shook her head, realizing she had done something awfully foolish and dangerous. "I was having these terrible dreams of a desert, and then I heard his voice in my head last night. I just wanted to make him stop. . . ."

"Nightmares!" Bauble cried. "I've been having them, too."

"Me too," Hugo added, frowning.

"Me three!" said Snabla.

"Clever of you to have deduced it was the work of Lord Carrion," Bauble told her.

"Oh! Thanks. . . ." Zelli felt a little sheepish. Bauble was usually the clever one. "He went on and on about some Lord of Death coming, and secrets hidden in the school's mountain, so I decided to do some digging of my own and that led me here." She gestured to the dormant door.

"And the nightmares?" Hugo asked, curving a talon under his chin nervously. "Will they stop?"

"I think so," Zelli replied. She grinned, not so sheepish now. "I threw a whole mess of tickling spiders on him—ought to teach him a lesson, don't you think?"

The others burst into laughter.

"Where did you find sssuch ssspidersss?" asked Snabla, still snorting and giggling.

"Some slaad kid left a jar of them in my locker trunk as a thank-you for helping with a bully," she explained. Zelli sometimes helped out the smaller, kinder, shier monster students, and as thanks they left her trinkets and treats in her trunk.

"Brilliant," Bauble laughed. "Less brilliant is facing a necromancer and skeletons on your own," Hugo pointed out.

"I forget sometimes that I don't have to do every-thing alone anymore," Zelli admitted. She held up the copy of *The Excavation of Akhellon Ridge* she had acquired. "This is what led me down here so quick-ly—I know I probably shouldn't listen to anything a necromancer says, but I think he was telling the truth. There's something hidden in the mountain, something he wants me to find."

"Taking orders from a necromancer?" Bauble snorted. "That doesn't sound like you."

Zelli grimaced. "I'm not taking orders from Lord Carrion! If there's something down here he wants, it would be better if we found it first. Then we can, I don't know, smash it or give it to the professors." Even just saying Lord Carrion's name aloud made her chilly all over. She made sure her fake horns and tail were in place. Wearing the disguise kept the other monsters at the school from realizing she wasn't a minotaur. It helped that her two mothers actually *were* minotaurs, and nobody wanted to risk angering them. "I know in my gut this isn't over, and if no one else is going to take it seriously, then I will."

"Now that *does* sound like you," Bauble replied.

"The professors have promised they will find a way to rescue the other students," Hugo reminded her. "We should really let them handle this."

"Who cares about ssstupid door in ssstinky pit?"

Snabla shouted, taking his torch and marching back away through the debris of the battle. "We are going to misss all the fun!"

"What fun?" Zelli asked, brow furrowed. The others began to wander away from the wall, though Bauble's eyes stayed glued to the design.

"Have you truly forgotten?" Hugo gave a deep chuckle. "The Tourney of Terror starts today."

"Oh, right," she said, adding a light laugh to make it convincing. "Of course. Of course I remembered."

She hadn't.

Just because one of Zelli's mothers was the Goreball coach didn't mean that Zelli had to enjoy the tournaments and games and pastimes that the other students of the Dungeon Academy cherished. With Snabla leading the way, they left behind the mysterious door, the kobold bouncing up and down impatiently, practically bouncing back toward the spiral staircase.

"Yesss! The Tourney of Terror!" Snabla stuck his narrow snout in the air and trilled. "We couldn't let you misss it, Zelli. The dragonsss will be here sssoon. The dragonsss are coming!"

3

"It really is a momentous occasion," Bauble explained. They had returned to their favored form: a big, heavy book with an elaborately illustrated cover, its swirls and curlicues artfully forming the mimic's eyes and wide mouth. It never ceased to amaze Zelli that mimics could turn into so many different things. "The Tourney of Terror comes but every fifty years, and the grand Goreball championship trophy weighs almost a hundred pounds!"

Zelli reached the top of the spiral staircase weary and dusty, but her companions remained energized by the promise of their rivals, the Waterdeep Dragons, arriving. The stairs dumped them out onto

the main floor of the far more trod, far brighter level, which was packed with classrooms. Here, all members of the Danger Club took History of Horrible Humans in a classroom to their right, where a floating skull, Professor Gast, droned on and on about despicable human adventures, past and present. It was, understandably, a bit of a touchy subject for Zelli, herself a human, and the daughter of a very famous, very despised-among-the-monster-community human, Allidora Steelstrike.

It was—*complicated*.

The last thing she wanted to think about was her birth mother—who would probably fall over in shock if she knew her daughter was about to willingly surround herself with chromatic dragons. Even the friendliest dragons, those who were shades of gold, silver, bronze, and all things shiny, were aloof, but green, black, red, white, and blue? Those dragons were cunning, vicious, and vile. It was no wonder they'd won the Tourney for the last zillion years (in truth it was more like three hundred, but to the students it felt like at least a zillion). Zelli herself had never met a dragon, but she had heard plenty of wild stories, most of them provided by Snabla, who fancied himself a dragon expert, and a creature related to drakes by blood. And of course, whenever he happened to get a fact wrong, Bauble was there to correct him. Even Bauble admitted that there was so much to know about dragons, even the wisest

professors at the academy knew only a fraction of all dragon lore. Dragons, after all, could live to be a thousand or more and guarded their secrets jealously.

Zelli glanced at each of her friends in turn, who were all in varying states of distraction, awe, and ecstasy with the Tourney of Terror looming. She couldn't blame them—life at the boarding school for monsters could become monotonous and dull, but while her friends were enamored with the upcoming cheering, heckling, snack snarfing, and celebrating, Zelli's mind remained fixed on the door-like etching in the dark pits beneath the school. More than that, she wanted to know what secrets lay beyond. Where did that strange door go? Did it even work? Who had put it there and why?

"Zelli?" Bauble grumbled. "Are you listening?"

"I'm all ears and horns," Zelli replied, shaking herself out of her wondering stupor. She wasn't ears or horns, but it was only polite to pay attention to Bauble, who seemed determined to give them all the full history of the Tourney of Terror.

They climbed yet another staircase, this one leading out of the dungeon levels for good. The air was visibly cleaner, brighter, and better smelling. Out in the main corridor, the hall monitor, a genie-like dao, drifted by, eyeing them for a moment before floating on her way, off to gleefully tattle on someone, no doubt.

A giant pendulum of an ax swung back and forth on the wall, clanging to announce the midday break.

Sitting tall, wide, and conspicuously empty along the wall across from them was the academy trophy case. It was hung with festive, hopeful banners of their mascot, the Dungeon Academy Flumph, a creature like a jolly bread loaf with ten eyestalks and jiggling tentacles. The case had been recently, presumptively dusted in what seemed to Zelli like a bit of a desperate attempt at lifting morale.

The Flumphs had never beaten the Waterdeep Dragons at . . . well, anything.

"How many times have the dragons won the Tourney exactly?" Zelli asked, smirking at the empty trophy case.

"Well. *Well.* The winner really isn't that important—" Bauble stammered.

"But the trophy weighs a hundred pounds," Zelli pointed out with a shrug. "So—"

"The symbolism is so much more meaningful than the sport itself," the mimic plowed on. The paisley designs of their eyebrows twitched fretfully. "Rival schools, a division of just two, coming together to commemorate unity and setting aside old grudges. Besides, it's not like we *couldn't* win. And wouldn't that be an amazing story? Who doesn't love an underblink-dog?"

"We will win!" Snabla assured them all, stuffing his now-snuffed-out torch under the strap hanging across his back. He hitched his scaled shield there, too. "I cannot wait to sssee the look on my cousin'sss face when we bash 'em and take the trophy!"

There was a momentary silence, followed by a communal groan.

"I ssswear it!" Snabla said, sticking his tongue out at them. "Oursss is the blood of dragonsss. You will all sssee!"

Snabla only referenced his alleged dragon cousin on even and odd days and on hours ending in "o'clock."

"Regardless," Bauble continued. "No matter the outcome of the tournament, we are all sure to learn so much from our dragon counterparts. Imagine all that

wisdom! Thousands and thousands of years of experience! They are sure to be horrid and nasty, and we can learn from that, too. Oh, but think of all the tricks we will learn to be better monsters!"

They trooped down the almost-empty corridor covered in a fine layer of pulverized bone and torch grease, clearly the last of the Dungeon Academy students to file out onto the field in search of Tourney of Terror delights. It was odd to see the school so deserted, more empty even than around the Baneday festivities or Mid-Never Winter break. And Zelli couldn't help but feel strange—she thought maybe the combined force of all their enthusiasm could bolster her spirits, but she still felt stuck, mired to the uneasy discovery she had made deep below the school.

"Professor Impro Vice assured me there would be healthy snacks and vegetables, too, not just sour glazed eyeballs and crispy bats," Hugo, who was a devotedly vegan owlbear, said softly, changing the subject. His hefty hand fell on Zelli's shoulder, startling her. "Zelli? Are you all right?"

"Mm. The Tourney is really exciting," she replied with a heavy sigh, sounding decidedly unexcited. "I'm not trying to ruin your fun, but I just can't stop thinking about the necromancer and the portal, and all the students we lost. Am I being silly?"

Hugo shook his head vehemently. "No! We are all

worried, Zelli. How could we not be?"

"In this book I found, it mentions the caves under the school are full of old secrets. There could be all sorts of hidden tunnels, and relics! Lord Carrion didn't seem very concerned to be our prisoner. What if he knows something we don't?"

"It does seem like an awfully big coincidence," Bauble admitted. They had almost reached the end of the corridor, overcast light pouring in through the windows on the doors leading out to the Goreball fields.

"The professors must hear about this," Zelli said, straightening up. There was no point sulking. Determination and purpose would get them a lot further than just worrying. "I have to tell them."

"Maybe they already know," Hugo suggested. "They have lived in this mountain a lot longer than we have. But we could talk to your mother; perhaps she can tell us more. . . ."

"Yesss! An exssscellent idea!" Snabla screeched, kicking open the doors with one mighty little clawed foot. "She will have the bessst ssseats for the match!"

Zelli rolled her eyes, but at least this way, everyone might get what they wanted—Zelli could assuage her lingering fears, and her friends would get a front-row view of the Goreball tournament. Her mother, Professor Stormclash, was the team overseer and planned all physical education at the school. And, as a minotaur,

she would be easy to spot in the crowd with her towering height and massive horns.

The screaming whistle helped, too.

It blew with deafening clarity just as the Danger Club stepped out onto the fresh, fragrant grass of the fields. Zelli moved toward the sound of that whistle in a daze, absorbed into a growing crowd of students, staff, and professors from the school. Slaadi, goblins, kobolds, bugbears, owlbears, myconid mushroom children, and more all crammed in along the sidelines while the Dungeon Academy Flumphs ran scrimmages on the main pitch. That game area opened up to the left, hemmed in by soaring trees, a seemingly endless forest that collared the grounds of the school, which rose behind them to a steep, high vanishing point at the top of the mountain. Ahead of them and to the right, spreading up to the edge of the tree line, lay the eager onlookers and the tents and carts built just for the Tourney of Terror.

For a brief moment, Zelli's concerns were forgotten. She had never seen anything like this in her entire life—she must have missed the stands going up, and the pennants that flapped and snapped in the wind, the smell of roasting meat and churned grass thick on the breeze. And she had never seen so many smiling, laughing monsters, rousing renditions of the academy's song chasing through the throng, bits of it here,

then picked up there, festive little horns tooting along to the words. . . .

We dwell! We're swell! We claw and roar and smell! We bump (in the night!), we thump (with a fright!), the DUNGEON ACADEMY FLUMPHS . . .

"Oh!" Hugo clapped his hands. "I smell popcorn!"

"We have to find my mother, remember?" Zelli held on to his wrist and dragged him through the crowd, threading around clusters of chatting, buzzing students. Snabla did not need to be convinced, hopping along ahead of them, drawn by Professor Stormclash's whistle.

"I sssee her! There ssshe isss!" Snabla darted away, much smaller than Zelli and Hugo. Particularly Hugo, who carried not only Bauble but also Flash, the blink dog hanging out of his backpack, licking the occasional monster on the head or cheek as they passed by.

As soon as they reached the edge of the rowdy crowd, Zelli found her mother presiding over the Goreball field, whistle clamped in her jaw, her intense, dark eyes surveying the field of play. Before any of the Danger Club could approach with a question, Professor Stormclash dropped the whistle out of her mouth and thundered, "Muckerson! Ugnar! That was sloppy! Look at Fearsmith, he's practically brain-dead thanks to you two! Get your heads in the game; the dragons will be here any minute!"

Her voice was powerful enough to shake the ground, and more than powerful enough to rattle the players sheepishly regrouping away from the gibbering mouther at center field. Zelli was no Goreball expert, but she had attended the school long enough to understand the rules. Two teams of eight monsters (or dragons) played up and down a long, narrow pitch. A wet, babbling mound of flesh and eyeballs known as a gibbering mouther started at the center, and to score, one had to lure that ball of gore down the field and across the opponent's goal line. Not so easily done, considering the gibbering mouther would do its very best to scream and wail so loudly it would trap anyone who dared go near. The wrangler positions corralled the mouther this way and that, while the shield-bearers deflected the wads of blinding goo spit out by the mouther. Smasher players were pretty self-explanatory, bashing into the opposing team, trying to distract them off course or knock a player into the churning mire around the mouther.

And Fresh Meat? Well, that was the most coveted and dangerous position of all. The one and only Fresh Meat on each team lured the gibbering mouther, keeping as close to it as possible without getting drawn into its maddening orbit. Players learned to withstand the horrible wailing and groaning, as earmuffs were strictly forbidden.

The first team to thirteen would be declared the winner, and if it happened to be a tie, Endless Sudden Death began, the teams playing until another goal was scored or everyone collapsed from exhaustion. According to Bauble, three Tourney of Terrors ago, the final game in the tournament went into Endless Sudden Death and lasted almost three days. The mimic had said this with stars in their eyes, but to Zelli it sounded a bit excessive.

Professor Stormclash had painted her curving minotaur horns gold and red for the occasion, matching the team colors. She caught sight of Zelli out of the corner of her eye and sidled toward them without ever tearing her gaze away from her players.

"Is it dire?" Professor Stormclash asked.

Not an unfair question considering Zelli had run away from school, trekked through an abandoned village, fought off wolves, reunited with her birth mother, and then defeated a necromancer all while she was supposed to be safely at school.

"I had some questions about something I found in the caves under the school—"

"—But you're all right?" At last, her mother spared her a quick look, eyes darting up and down, checking for flesh wounds. "You're in one piece? No broken bones? Curses? Hexes?"

"I'm fine, Mom, I just—"

"Zelli, you know I don't have time for this right now." It wasn't like Professor Stormclash to ignore her, but Zelli knew the stakes were high. Zelli withered, hanging her head. Goreball was fun, sure, but an impending necromantic threat seemed like a much higher priority. "Stay out of the caves, sweetheart, they're dangerous. You're not supposed to be down there for a reason."

"But there were skeletons down there, and if you could just tell me what you know about—"

"—Probably one of Gast's experiments gone awry. Honey, stay out of the caves. I shouldn't need to give you another reason besides 'there are skeletons.'" She managed another swift glance at Zelli, noticing then that she was with Hugo, Snabla, Bauble, and Flash. "Why don't you go find something to eat? The vendors will be swarmed soon. Try to enjoy the day, Zelli. Please? Please enjoy something that doesn't involve swinging your sword."

Zelli wondered what she must look like, a puny human girl wearing fake horns and a tail, glaring up into a real minotaur's face with her hands on her hips and her lips in a pout. Comically suspicious, no doubt, to anyone willing to take a close look at her. But not even her mother was looking at her anymore.

"Mom, this is important to me," Zelli whispered.

"And *this* is important to *me*," her mother replied.

Then she ruffled Zelli's thick black hair gently and said, "We will discuss this soon. The Tourney will be over in a matter of days. Now, promise me you'll enjoy the festivities. Promise."

Professor Stormclash knelt, held out her giant, muscular hand, her fingertips pinched together to make a circle. Biting down hard on her cheek in frustration, Zelli mimicked the gesture, then bumped her hand against her mother's. She made sure to hide her other hand behind her back, two fingers twined together to cancel out the vow. "Fine. I promise."

Zelli had chosen to stay in this world of monsters, chosen to stay with Kifin and Iasme Stormclash, the minotaur mothers who had raised her, and choosing someone like that was powerful. Why couldn't she see that Zelli was just trying to protect them?

"Wonderful." Professor Stormclash stood tall again, nodding toward the assembled friends behind Zelli. "Hello, Hugo. Hello, Bauble. Snabla."

The rest of the Danger Club had stars in their eyes when Zelli turned away. Her mother had become a full-blown celebrity for the duration of the Tourney of Terror, it seemed. Zelli grunted and dug her elbow into Hugo's side. "Come on," she mumbled. "Let's get you that popcorn."

"Yes!" Hugo hissed, pumping his fist. "I mean . . . are you sure? You don't look very happy, Zelli."

"I'm probably just overreacting." Zelli fell into step behind Snabla again, who couldn't wait to march them back through the shoulder-to-shoulder sea of students and toward the food. *But I'm definitely not,* Zelli thought. *Everyone else has their heads in the clouds, not me.*

Even sure of herself, Zelli found it hard not to be enchanted by the tents, the banners, the cheering, bubbly throngs of monsters in their red-and-gold memorabilia. She glanced up at Hugo as they snaked their way to the back of the stands, where a row of tattered flumph-themed tents waited. The owlbear beamed—grinning and laughing in a way she had never seen. His eyes sparkled as he grabbed her arm in excitement, hooting and pointing toward one cart in particular. A spotted troll wrapped in a striped Flumphs scarf hummed excitedly behind a steaming cauldron, popcorn kernels pinging off the burning-hot pewter like sleet bouncing off a cobblestone road.

Hugo trotted over to the vendor, returning a moment later with shining eyes and a beak full of food.

"Look!" Bauble shrieked. "I want to see what they have!"

Not far down the lane, a few muscle-bound gnolls hammered together the last posts for the flumph-themed tent. Red-and-gold streamers hung from every post, the brownish canvas riddled with holes

and the banner flying above it stained, but still somehow proud. Zelli struggled to keep up with her friends as they pelted toward the tent, Snabla reaching it ahead of the others and diving headfirst into a pile of freshly woven tunics. Hugo crammed the last of his popcorn into his beak before trying on a replica of the flumph uniform—a red jerkin with gold spikes and the school crest boldly displayed on the front.

"Look! I've changed my binding to match!" Bauble declared. And indeed, the mimic had rearranged their cover, the scrollwork along the spine and cover all done in crimson and glittering jewels.

"That's impressive, Bauble. You look perfect now," Zelli told them, hating the lack of interest in her voice. Snabla managed to leap up in the air and loop a scarf around Zelli's neck before she meandered away from her giggling friends. She was accustomed to feeling like the odd one out—after all, she was a human girl masquerading as a minotaur at a school for monsters—but this was harder somehow. Feeling apart from her friends, separated by a barrier she couldn't describe, felt worse. Why couldn't she just let go and have fun?

Her stubbornness, her insistence on following her

heart, was something her mothers had always been proud of, and she wasn't about to give up on it now. Standing at the edge of the tent, she gazed out at the next structure down the lane. There, not a single post was crooked, not a stain in sight, no puny banners or anemic pennants fluttering in the wind—no, it was all pin straight, neat, orderly, and above all? Regal.

The Waterdeep Dragon memorabilia tent was constructed of thick, lacquered poles, the canvas sparkling white. Purple and white silk fluttered from the scalloped edges of the canvas, a dream of soft, sumptuous fabric, like the tales of knights and maidens. Tales, of course, that she was supposed to find silly and repulsive. But a weak corner of her human heart responded to it, and she sighed.

Then she noticed a bugbear dressed in red-and-gold armor and a furred collar tiptoeing toward the Waterdeep Dragons' vendor tent. Zelli recognized her at once—it was Patty, a student who they had saved from Lord Carrion and his army of undead in the cave outside Horntree Village. As Zelli watched silently, the bugbear glanced nervously in every direction, then turned, scrunched up her face, and pulled down her trousers, mooning the tent. She snort-laughed and pulled up her pants, then started to shuffle away. Zelli could hear her friends screaming with laughter in the line for Grubs on a Stick.

"Patty!" Zelli called.

The bugbear froze, eyes blasting wide. Then she saw Zelli hurrying toward her and relaxed, crossing her arms over her chest and puffing a piece of tawny fur out of her face.

"What do you want, runt?" she snarled.

Oh. Zelli had forgotten—the dean had sent all the students involved in the Horntree Village incident to Nihildris, the counselor mind flayer. Any "troubling" or "problematic" or "horrifically paralyzing and trau- matizing" experiences could be erased. It seemed that Nihil- dris had also erased Zelli's heroics from Patty's mind, too. The bugbear had no idea that she was glaring down at one of her saviors.

"Forget it." Zelli shrugged. "I, um, I thought that was hilarious. You're so cool."

Patty rolled her eyes. "Yeah. Obviously. Tell Zxati- cus and you're dead, runt."

The bugbear shouldered Zelli out of the way, swag- gering back to her friends.

"Got it," Zelli groused under her breath. "You have a good day, too, gnomeface."

When it came time for Nihildris to wipe the mem- ories of the Danger Club, Professor Stormclash had intervened, arguing that they had not been abducted, but had gone to save the students of their own free will, implying not a scary experience but a fearless one. They were at the academy to learn, after all, and their skills had increased exponentially by battling a real live necromancer. They were better monsters for having ventured into the unknown and survived. After a prolonged interview with both Dean Zxaticus and the mind flayer, the Danger Club were deemed "relatively unscathed" by the incident, and they were allowed to keep their memories. Zelli would never forget how disappointed Nihildris seemed after being denied the pleasure of brain-wiping her and her friends.

Zelli noticed a familiar shape in the distance, beyond the Waterdeep Dragons' tent—a large, fleshy orb floating near the ground. The sun had just peeked out from behind a bank of clouds, making the beholder's many eyes glint and flash. Dean Zxaticus and a whole procession of teachers were making their way toward the field. Zxaticus led the way, draped somewhat awkwardly in a red-and-gold sash. Zelli made her decision in a snap, darting away from the clearing and toward the dean.

"Dean! Zxaticus! Sir!" Zelli was out of breath by the time she stumbled up to the beholder. His dozens of eyes swiveled toward her in unison. Zxaticus was an intimidating presence on an average day, but with the

professors arranged behind him like flanking guards, he was even more imperious. The little lids on his eyes lowered, and he squinted at her, a glare that could stop a charging centaur.

"Yes, Stormclash?" he drawled.

"I . . . Skeletons, sir. Skeletons! I believe there's some kind of door in the caves below the school! I found it in a book, then when I went to investigate, I was attacked by skeletons! Find that odd? Coincidental, maybe? And the necromancer! I mean, should we not . . ." Zelli wasn't a rambler, but she couldn't help it, standing there in the shadow of the beholder, a phalanx of stone-silent professors studying her, the words scattered out artlessly, breathlessly. She wasn't brave (or stupid) enough to admit that she had figured out where they were holding Lord Carrion and managed to sneak in and speak to him.

"Skeletons?" Zxaticus sighed.

"Y-Yes. Yes, sir," Zelli replied, shrinking.

"In the caves?"

"That's right."

Now she could only see a sliver of eyeball on each eyestalk. *Uh-oh.*

"In the caves that are *forbidden*?"

Zelli clasped her hands behind

her back and rocked on her feet, dropping her eyes to the grass darkened by the floating beholder's shadow. "It . . . it just seemed important."

"More important than following the rules?" Zxaticus began to drift by, his eyes rotating to face forward as she was brushed aside. "Perhaps the caves are forbidden because there are things there you need not concern yourself with, Zellidora."

Zelli wanted to grab the beholder by the tentacles and shake him. How could that be the reply? Why didn't anyone take her concerns seriously? So what if she was just a student? And why, for the love of all that was monstrous, did rules matter more than thwarting the plans of dangerous necromancers?

Opening her mouth to say something that would surely get her expelled, Zelli cried out, almost toppling over into the grass. The forest around them shook, the trees moaning and creaking, bending from a sudden blasting gust. There was a rhythm to the wind, steady and hypnotic, like the heartbeat of the world itself. No . . . not a heartbeat. *Wings.* The force and fury of a hundred pairs of wings . . .

The Waterdeep Dragons had arrived.

4

The sky filled with a stunning blaze of colors—red, blue, green, ebony, and white blurs that became clearer and clearer as the dragons descended in a careful formation. Zelli found her friends among the assembled students on the rickety stands running alongside the field. The scrimmaging flumphs froze, all heads furry, scaled, gooey, bumpy, and smooth tilted back to admire the arrival of the Waterdeep Dragons.

The Danger Club had managed to carve out a little corner of the right-most stand, wedged between two groups of myconid students, whose soft mushroom bodies scattered clouds of spores in excitement. Zelli batted away a haze of mushroom funk and settled in beside Hugo.

"What a display!" he cried. "Magnificent!"

"My cousssin will be leading them all!" Snabla shouted, raising his fists in the air and cackling.

"Oh, that's just nonsense, Snabla," Bauble immediately corrected him, still in the form of a large book emblazoned with red, gold, and the school's flumph mascot. "That black dragon at the front would be their dean. Allegedly, she's thousands of years old. Can you imagine?"

"What are they doing now?" Hugo asked as Flash bounced eagerly on his lap. "It looks like a formation. . . ."

"The school's crest! Yes! That must have taken days of practice." It was hard to make out Bauble's voice over all the booing. Even if the display was impressive, perhaps beautiful, the Dungeon Academy students weren't going to give them the satisfaction of admiration. Besides, nobody wanted to get detention for excessive sportsmanship. This was a chance for everyone, from the smallest myconid kid to the largest gnoll, to show how awful and horrid they could be.

Zelli shielded her eyes against the wan sunlight, watching silently as the hundreds of dragons filling the air above the field carefully glided into the shape of their school crest. The thick band of trees making up the Endless Forest shook, hard, then gradually a gap appeared, widening into an expanding tunnel. The quaking sent Bauble tumbling out of Hugo's backpack, but the owlbear managed to catch them before the mimic landed on the students below.

 47

Even Zelli lurched back and forth in her seat to the rhythm of the shaking and shivering and splintering. Just as she was sure the stands would rattle apart and send the whole school sprawling to the ground, an immense green dragon appeared through the tunnel in the forest, each plodding step booming through Zelli's chest like a roll of thunder.

"I wonder where they'll stay! Not in our dormitories, I don't think; how would they fit?" Bauble wondered aloud. They had struck up a constant stream of questions and facts running softly under the jeers and taunts of the crowd. The sheer chaos and cacophony of it all was beginning to make Zelli's head spin. Bauble did their very best to be heard, continuously drowned out by the litany of insults about mothers, gold hordes, and fancy scales. "Do you think they brought an altar to Tiamat? And do you see that? White dragons! They almost never leave snowy climes...."

Meanwhile, the green dragon marching out of the forest, wizened with age, had its eyes closed as it pulled a flat cart behind it, the platform laden with tents of marvelous shapes, a veritable white-and-purple tent city emerging. Finished with their aerial performance, the chromatic dragons circling above flew faster and faster, diving down toward one another until they formed a dizzying funnel, a vortex that dipped down toward the previously scrimmaging, now-frozen Flumphs. The team scattered, shouting, a blast of wind like a tornado slamming into the stands. Zelli yelped, watching a tiny first-year kobold fly end over end out of the stands.

Zelli herself just managed to catch her false horns before they, too, were carried away by the wing-whipped wind. Nobody noticed, as there were far more exciting things to behold.

As the dragons racing down from the sky neared the ground, the students in the stands held a collective breath, bracing. But the massive collision they had all anticipated never came. Perhaps the most impressive feat was that they all managed to land with utmost delicacy, hardly disturbing a blade of grass as they alighted, and waited for applause that never came.

Except from Snabla. The pointy little kobold was a Flumph in team colors only, convinced of his dragon's blood and dragon's heart. Hugo quickly and gently lowered Snabla's clapping claws before any of the larger bullies noticed the kobold cheering whole-heartedly for their rivals.

A handful of large dragons emerged from the forest behind the green one, some toting carts filled with folded canvas, some carrying what appeared to be monstrously large haunches of raw meat. Zelli heard Hugo gag with revulsion. The Dungeon Academy

staff processed toward the field, where the dragon in the lead, a majestic ebony creature with silvery-white eyes and twisty horns, waited somberly.

The tunnel that had opened in the Endless Forest vanished, the trees knitting themselves back together to create a solid, unbroken wall of trunks. Right where that opening had been, Zelli watched a new phenomenon occur—a portal. She was rather familiar with their appearance now, having thrown herself headlong into necromantic research in the library, and having closed a real one with her friends when they faced down and thwarted Lord Carrion. Leaping to her feet, she nearly screamed. Hugo tugged on her sleeve.

"Shh, the dragons are going to speak!" he whispered.

But Zelli knew what she was looking at. She had never been so sure in her life. The jagged glowing ring hovered just off the ground near the forest. And now the blasted professors were walking right across her field of vision, obscuring the portal, which lay not terribly far from the back of the white-and-purple tent offering Waterdeep Dragon scarves and tunics.

"Do you see what I do?" she asked, spinning to find her friends completely ignoring her.

"Keep it down," Bauble muttered, their eyes fixed on the Goreball field. "I want to hear every word!"

A row of bugbears in red-and-gold school liveries marched alongside the professors, pausing, turning almost in unison, and then lifting dented brass horns to their mouths. They honked out a fanfare, and Zelli winced, covering her ears. She stared a moment longer at Hugo, Bauble, and Snabla, but it was clear they weren't interested.

"Isn't that strange?" she asked. Nobody responded. She sighed, adding: "I never thought I'd see six rows of naked, dancing bugbears in the forest!" Nothing. With a huff, she climbed out of the stands, much to the vocal chagrin of the myconids whose views of the event she temporary—outrageously!—obstructed. Dean Zxaticus's voice boomed off woods and mountain as Zelli raced away from the stands, dodging behind the Waterdeep Dragons' vendor tent and toward the glimmer of shimmering pink near the tree line. She passed under the shadow of the tall, looming green dragon, who didn't seem to notice the human down on the ground trotting by.

Her hands balled up into tight fists; she wanted so badly to be enchanted by it all, to have the freedom of heart and mind to be thrilled, awed, and completely immersed in flumph team pride, but the sour feeling in her gut wouldn't let up. Her birth mother, Allidora Steelstrike, the Unyielding Blade, was a famous, bold adventurer, a woman who battled untold dangers alone. That was in her blood, but she had also been raised by two fiercely loving, strong, and protective minotaurs. With all that ferocity coursing through her, how could her gut instinct be wrong?

If this is nothing, she promised herself, *I'll give up on this wild gibberling hunt and try to make the most of the Tourney of Terror.*

There! A reasonable compromise. Bauble would be proud. She had to imagine Bauble would also be proud if this portal turned out to be something significant. Her friends would come back down to Faerûn eventually, once their minds weren't soaring sky high with the dragons.

I knew it. Zelli watched as the glowing pink oval hovering near the trees grew sharper and realer. It hummed with a low, hypnotic thrum.

"Attention, all! Attention, all!" Dean Zxaticus thundered.

But Zelli's attention was extremely elsewhere, on a dark lump rooting around at the base of the portal.

It was something . . . alive. Moving. Frantically shivering. . . . Zelli slowed her pace, breathing deeply, steadying her hands as she reached back and drew her practice sword. One good thump and she would apprehend the portal maker.

Lord Carrion's scratching rasp of a voice seared across her brain. *You can delay me, but you cannot delay the inevitable. More will come; more will come in service of my lord.*

Was this the arrival of that foretold lord?

Zelli brought down her sword hard on the wiggling lump of robes. Instead of collapsing, the thing leapt to its feet, spun, a dark cloak falling backward.

"Ouch! That really hurt!"

Sword raised above her head again, Zelli stared in panicked confusion. The shimmering purply-pink portal behind him disappeared, vanishing with a muted *pop*. It wasn't a foul, cackling necromancer or a heap of reanimated skeletons, but a boy.

A *human* boy.

Zelli gasped. "But you're . . . you're a . . . *human*," she blurted. And he was indeed that, dressed in a simple red tunic over baggy brown trousers, a long black belt knotted around his waist.

The boy—her age, perhaps, or a bit older—seemed to notice something in the grass by her feet. His eyes widened, and he dropped down, snatching up a glint of gold there. An amulet. He stood, brushing mud and leaves off the radiant necklace.

"You've got quite an arm, *minotaur*," he muttered, tying the jewel around his neck. The moment he did, Zelli had to blink, not believing her eyes. He was no longer just a reedy blond boy in a grubby tunic . . . no, in a puff of smoke, he had become a *real* red dragon. A bit larger than a pony, he sat on his haunches in the wet grass and the shade of the forest, regarding her with his narrow head tilted to the side.

"But . . . But no. You're a human! I saw it!" She almost darted forward to touch his scaly nose and make sure it was real. Then she remembered that red dragons were greedy and unpredictable and took a step back.

"Are you sure?" His golden eyes narrowed, then slid side to side nervously. "I mean . . . maybe you imagined it. That's it. You definitely imagined it. No, I've been a dragon all this time!" He dropped his head back and laughed, a wisp of smoke curling from his nostrils. His gaze narrowed further as he inspected her. "What are you doing here anyway?"

"Stop asking me questions!" Zelli barked, lowering her sword but not sheathing it. This was all too strange for her to feel safe. "I asked you first! What did that

amulet do? Why don't you look like a human boy any-more? I know what I saw. You're not a red dragon, just a boy in a red shirt!"

The jet of steam from his nose rose now in rings. "Hey," he growled. "At least mine is convincing."

Zelli reached up and felt her horns, finding they were noticeably askew.

"Oh," she whispered.

"Oh indeed," the dragon laughed. "I've never seen a minotaur with such shoddy horns."

She couldn't argue. Her crooked horns and felt tail couldn't hold a candle to the blazing torch of his disguise. Zelli pointed to the white-and-purple-striped scarf around his dragon neck. "How did you fool a bunch of dragons into letting you into their school?"

"I'm not telling you anything," he sniffed, superior.

"Oh." Zelli rolled her eyes. "Typical dragon. Arrogant and selfish. Well, if you aren't will-ing to give me answers, I'll let all the professors know you were poking around a strange portal. Seems awfully suspicious to me. They'll want to know why you're fiddling with dark magics on school grounds. Purple wibbly portals like that mean one thing to me—necromancers. I should know. I fought one and lived to tell of it!"

Ha, let him be arrogant now.

At that, the dragon's eyes flew open.

"Wait just a moment. You know of the battle at Horntree Cavern?"

"Know of it? I was there!" Zelli knew it was unwise to boast, but he seemed genuinely impressed. He stared at her with renewed interest. "How did you hear about it?"

"There were rumors," the dragon replied slowly. "But nobody at my school really believed a bunch of little monsters could defeat an actual necromancer and his army of undead. . . ."

Zelli was about to bite out a smart response when he added, "But I see I was in error. The rumors are true, and you must be one of the more formidable monsters at this academy."

She lifted her chin. "Don't you mean formidable human?"

The red dragon snorted. "Maybe I do, though it would be too painful to say."

"But you *are* a human. Just tell me the truth," Zelli gritted out between clenched teeth. "You can trust me. We're both humans masquerading as something

we're not. I won't tell anyone your secret. I just want to understand!"

"I'm not . . ." The dragon propped himself onto all fours, then let out a hard puff of steam from his nose. "Fine. *Fine.* Just lower that sword, please, I'd like to avoid another nasty thump. It's . . . my story is a long tale and right now it's not for the telling."

"And why is that?" Zelli demanded.

"Because we're not alone." The dragon nodded to the space behind her, and Zelli glanced over her shoulder to find two red dragons, slightly larger than the masquerading human, join them in the clearing.

"Looks like Truescale's got a lizard chaser," one of them hissed. He was missing his right ear, the scars from that wound running jaggedly down across his forehead and above his eye. Snarling, he inspected Zelli from horns to boots. Either she was mistaken, or that dragon looked ready to devour her as a light snack. "Just what are you supposed to be?"

"A kobold or something, I'll wager," the other one sneered, equally venomous. She was a long, elegant creature, with a sinuous, flicking tail that seemed to have a mind of its own, as she sized up Zelli and then went to stand conspicuously close to "Truescale."

"Kobolds don't have horns, bogbreath," Zelli said, backing away and stuffing her sword back into the scabbard strapped to her shoulders. She was brave,

but not pick-a-fight-with-three-dragons brave.

"Oh, it talks," said the girl dragon, snorting. "Adorable. Forgive me for not recognizing your kind; I'm not in the habit of studying lesser creatures."

"Is there a reason you're here?" the human . . . dragon . . . boy . . . asked. He didn't seem pleased at their arrival and immediately began creating distance between them.

"Just wondering where you scampered off to," the scarred dragon replied. He wouldn't stop glaring at Zelli, and it was making her itch with irritation. Who did they think they were, acting like they were better than her? She bet they would squeal like baby boars and run into the woods if they knew she had two minotaurs and a famous adventurer for parents.

"I, uh, saw something strange over here by the edge of the trees, behind our tents," Truescale explained, his gaze shifting rapidly to Zelli, his eyes boring into hers as if begging her not to reveal what she had seen.

"Saw something strange, Tavian?" the girl asked, nodding toward Zelli. "Like this gangled varmint?"

"I'm a *minotaur*," Zelli bit out, stuffing the urge to draw her sword and teach the imperious dragon a truly unforgettable lesson in manners.

"Sure. And I'm a Lord of the Nine," the girl muttered, blowing impatiently on her gleaming claws.

"Leave her alone," Tavian Truescale sighed, leading

the other two red dragons away from Zelli, and away from the site of the mysterious, vanishing portal. "It was nothing after all. Right, minotaur? Just . . . a trick of the eye."

Zelli didn't miss his interesting choice of words. A trick of the eye. Did he mean the portal or himself? And were they supposed to be allies or something?

"You're missing all the good stuff," the scarred dragon insisted, flapping. "Did you know one of their professors is a human stuck in a gelatinous cube? Ridiculous! What could a half-digested human teach? Advanced Rotting? Introduction to Decomposition? You should get away from that creature before anyone thinks you might like its company."

The scarred dragon and the pretty one apparently thought that was the funniest quip they had ever heard, dissolving into huffs and giggles. But the human in disguise ignored them, following a few paces behind.

"Ignore them, they're awful. Later," Tavian Truescale told Zelli in a whisper, his golden eyes flashing. "I shall find you later."

She nodded, once, and briefly watched the insufferable trio wander away. But Zelli wasn't done wondering about the portal she had seen. Somehow, it made her feel better and less alone knowing the dragon boy had seen the phenomenon, too. Her pride might have been bruised but her resolve remained hearty, and she

returned to where she was sure the glimmer of pink and purple had been. Kneeling in the grass, she found the depression where Tavian had searched for his amulet. And she found something more.

Tracks. They did not belong to a boy or a dragon, but to something with such defined ridges that for a moment the image did not make sense. Zelli felt the air around her tighten and contract as she finally recognized what it might be. If she looked closely enough, she could see the bones dented into the earth, proof of a skeletal visitor, one that had come from that ominous portal.

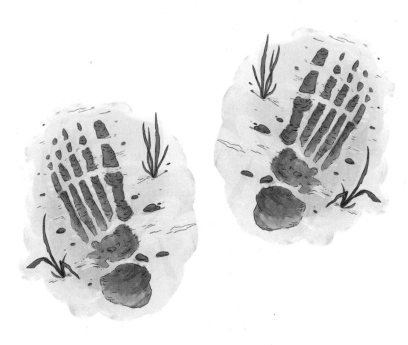

5

The next morning, Zelli stared into her porridge as if it were a magic mirror that held all the answers. There was nothing there but honey, slop, and milk. Most of the students took breakfast either in their rooms or the dining chamber, but with classes out for the duration of the tournament, Zelli had decided to visit her mothers that morning, crossing the misty, dew-laden grounds to the staff housing where Kifin and Iasme Stormclash lived. She had felt the damp creep up her boots and into her bones as she hurried to the house with the big wooden door, cyclops workers visible across the Goreball pitch as they set up the tents and structures hauled to the Dungeon Academy by the dragons. She had slept fitfully, but not because of nightmares. Lord Carrion had left her alone, but her mind was too full of worries to allow for peaceful slumber. Overnight, a veritable village had sprung up along the edge of the forest, great elevated

roosts of strong timber, rope, and canvas hoisted into place by the hulking cyclops groundskeepers.

In that lifting gloom, the school and the day had seemed almost mythic, with the sun's first fingers visible above the tree line, huge silhouettes moving slowly through the fog, the outline of a dragon visible through the tents, lit from within by roaring braziers. Zelli had stopped in the grass and watched, hands in her trouser pockets to keep them warm, wondering if there was a necromancer hiding somewhere in the shadows that morning sought to banish.

Then she'd gone on her way, and ducked into the familiar smell of wood smoke, herbs, and leather, the smells of her childhood and her mothers. There was always a bowl of porridge ready for her, on the off chance she wanted to eat there, fresh from the cauldron bubbling over the hearth.

"Did you come to eat or to brood?" Iasme asked. She was slighter than Professor Stormclash, though still giant by almost any standards. Despite her size, Iasme was deft enough with a needle, and darned socks and tunics and woolly cloaks for professors and students, bringing in a little extra coin to supplement the professor's wages. Iasme sat at the head of the table, while Kifin paced near the hearth, a sheaf of parchment trailing from her hands. Goreball formations. It was only a small cottage, three rooms with a spare dirt

floor, crocheted rugs, mismatched chairs, and burlap for curtains, but Zelli had liked it that way. It always felt overstuffed like a well-loved chair, crowded, filled up with beating hearts.

"You said we would talk about what I found under the school," Zelli insisted, turning her wooden spoon slowly in the porridge. *Should I tell them about what Lord Carrion said? No, it will just make them worry more. Besides, he's chained up and the dreams have stopped; he can't hurt me now. . . .*

That brought Kifin Stormclash's pacing to a halt. She swiveled her curling horns and bullish snout around and returned to the table, placing both mighty fists on the wood. It creaked. "You're right. I did say that. So, what did you find?"

Zelli blinked up at her. "Really?"

"Yes, really. We always listen to each other in this family. What worries you worries me, Zellidora. What did you want to tell me?"

She almost knocked over her bowl in her excitement. "I, um, found this book on the history of the school. There's a whole cave system underneath the academy, and dragons lived there for a while, then necromancers." At that, Kifin cocked one furry black eyebrow. "Yes. I know. Necromancers. Really! And I found this sketch of a door in the book, and then when I went down there to look myself, it was there. It's definitely a door, but I couldn't see a way to open it, and it was guarded by a whole army of skeletons!"

"Zellidora Keenfury Stormclash, if you are fibbing right now . . ."

"I swear I'm not!" Zelli dug quickly in the book bag near her feet and produced the book, opening to a strip of tunic she had used to mark the correct page. "See? That looks just like a door, doesn't it? There's no way to open it, but it must be guarding something important! If you turn it this way, doesn't the design look just like necromantic runes? Lord Carrion's robes had something similar. . . ."

"I see." Kifin shared a look with Iasme, then dragged a hand over her face slowly. "And just how did you defeat an army of skeletons by yourself?"

 66

"Well, I didn't. Not really. My friends helped. That part is not important! The dean won't listen to me. Nobody will listen to me. . . ." Zelli's shoulders slumped with exhaustion and frustration. "I know something is wrong about this. Yesterday I saw what looked like a portal in the clearing, and an odd footprint. What if we're all in terrible danger?"

Kifin reached across the table and engulfed Zelli's small human hand in hers.

"This does sound serious."

Zelli's jaw fell. "It . . . does? It does. You're going to help?"

"Let me speak to the dean myself. He has a lot to juggle with the Tourney of Terror and the dragons visiting, but I won't let this slip through the cracks." Kifin let go of her hand and picked up her Goreball formations again. "Have I heard you?"

Zelli nodded, shoveling porridge into her mouth before flying out the door. "You heard me!"

The Danger Club had to know about this. And the portal. And Tavian Truescale. Zelli almost tripped over her bootlaces as she streamed across the pitch, as fast, lethal, and determined as a Goreball player. There was so much to tell them! Bauble would know more about the transformation that boy had made to become a dragon. Maybe it had everything to do with that amulet he wore.

It was a pale, ghastly hour when she reached the cavernous main corridor of the school within the mountain. From down the hall, the pendulous old great ax of the Mad Smithy clanged one hour past dawn. The bats nestled in the beams above her remained awake and watchful, their eyes glittering in the torchlight, following her, red and shining like the wet gleam of fish eggs. Not a soul stirred in the hall, not even the ever-present, ever-vigilant dao hall monitor, Jizek. Zelli's footsteps rippled out ahead of her, noisy even to her own ears. She wondered who of her friends would be up first. Probably Bauble, although Hugo liked to get an early start and make dandelion-root tea before his day began.

She expected to find a professor or two awake and drifting through the halls, but she did not expect to nearly collide with a dragon as they came trundling out of the dining chamber. Zelli yelped. Tavian snorted. She bounced off his iron-hard scales and landed with a wince on her backside. His half-eaten frog skewer landed in her lap. Grumbling, she jumped to her feet and handed him the rest of his breakfast.

"What are you doing in here?" she asked, annoyed. Then suspicious. Then annoyed *and* suspicious. "Are you even allowed inside our school?"

"'Our' school, is it?" Tavian hoisted an inquisitive brow ridge. He ate the last frog off the skewer and

 68

incinerated the stick with a blast of fiery breath. Zelli
started, narrowly avoiding the gust of flames.

"Well, it's not *yours*."

"No, but I can't figure how it's yours, either," Tavian replied. She noticed a weird glimmering bit of goo
on the scales of his shoulder. Probably a spitball from
some passing wise guy. "I know your sort aren't keen
on sportsmanship, etiquette, grace, or delicacy, but
even for a 'monster' this is a cold welcome. Are we not
all here in the spirit of the Tourney? Of unity?"

Zelli cocked her hip to the side, resting one fist on
it. "Unity? Your kind are known for cheating, lying,

stealing, hoarding, and let's not forget eating sheep and villagers for a midday snack. How many farms have you burned down so far today, hmm?"

"Today? None, but the day is young." Tavian stepped back and laughed, then lowered his head and neck in a formal bow. "My name is Tavian Truescale. I came looking for you, as I vowed I would."

She twitched her lips back and forth nervously. "Yeah, all right. Glad you did. I'm Zelli. Zellidora Stormclash."

"Quite the name," he observed, straightening up. "Sounds like it comes with an impressive pedigree."

You have no idea, scale-face.

"You were kidding about the farm stuff, right?" she asked.

"More or less."

"Now that we're done with all the polite stuff, I want to know how you . . ." Zelli trailed off, glancing in every direction. With her luck, Jizek would be lurking somewhere around the corner, just waiting to listen in on their conversation. "How *you* . . . are *you.*"

"A story for a story," he replied, gesturing down the corridor with his clawed forepaw. "Where were you destined?"

"The dormitories," Zelli told him, falling into step beside him. "But be careful and follow my lead. There are traps everywhere."

His lip curled. "Naturally."

"Are you allowed to spend time with me?" Zelli asked, curious. The other dragons that had happened upon them in the clearing had not seemed fond of monsters, to say the least. She felt a little smug that her "shoddy" disguise had fooled those jerks.

"Allowed?" Tavian snorted. "I do as I please. Besides, I'm much more interested in you and the Battle of Horntree Cavern than a bunch of snotty lizards. They treat everyone terribly, even me. They've just adjusted their aim now that there are so-called 'lesser' creatures to pick on."

"You want to spend time with monsters?" Zelli asked, eyes wide. "Seems strange."

"I think we have established that we are both that."

She shrugged and nodded. He seemed different from the other dragons—much nicer, at the very least. "True. My birth mother is a human adventurer. A Steelstrike. She didn't want me to follow in her footsteps, you know, lead a life of slaying and dungeon delving. She tried to give me away, thinking a family of nice farmers would find me." Zelli laughed and shook her head. "Only . . . it was a family of nice minotaurs who found me. Not exactly what my birth mother had in mind, but they take good care of me. I wear the tail and horns to fit in. It's not so bad. I've found some friends, and I do my best not to stand out too much."

Tavian nodded along with her story, doing as she did to avoid the pressure-rigged floor stones that would trigger a barrage of poisoned darts. His size made for slow going. While there were many larger monsters at the school, few rivaled the size and bulk of an adolescent dragon. "And do these friends, the other heroes of Horntree Cavern, know your secret?"

"They do," Zelli admitted. She couldn't wait to see the look on Snabla's face when he heard a dragon had called him a hero. "They accept me for me."

He went quiet. For a moment she wondered if he was offended. Then he made a strange, strangled sound, like a gurgle. He coughed to cover it. "How . . . fortunate."

"What's your story, dragon boy?"

"As I said, it's long and winding," he replied, pausing to gaze up at the ax of the Mad Smithy as it swung back and forth on the wall. The chests students used for storage lined the corridor, many carved with stick figures or obscenities. One, no doubt belonging to a myconid student, read: BEWARE THE FART KING.

"Does it look like anyone is awake? Go ahead," Zelli told him. "Hey, don't be nervous. Remember? I'm a kid wearing fake horns and a woolly tail, so I'm the last to judge."

Tavian's pointy shoulders drew back at that, and his chin lowered. "As you've surmised, I was born a

human. We lived in a speck of a village in the western heartlands. When I was but three, a drought came that lasted long enough to ruin the whole valley. One day, a rich traveler came through the village and noticed their plight. He wanted to ease their suffering, and so my parents gave me away." He paused again, this time inspecting another student's locker trunk. A fanged goblin had been carved there.

"They just let a stranger take you?" Zelli gasped. "That's awful."

"It was a traveling dragonborn sorcerer who offered to care for me, and they couldn't resist. There was no food and no work, and I was but a drain upon them. I have to believe they were on starvation's doorstep; how else could one explain trusting a stranger?"

Zelli herself had never met or seen a dragonborn in person, though she knew from her studies of human-oid adventurers that they looked very much like the spawn of dragons and humans. They hatched from eggs, had talons, and stood quite tall; they walked on two feet like she did, but they also had scales in many colors like any dragon might.

"Elgred Morbide was his name, and he promised I would be well looked after—fed, clothed, even edu-cated. He sensed I had a gift for magic, and no doubt filled their heads with wild possibilities. I'm sure they still expect me to ride back into the village on a white

73

horse, my magical exploits the talk of the Sword Coast."
Tavian sighed and scratched at his chin with one dark
red claw. Without realizing it, Zelli had slowed her
pace to a crawl, fascinated by the boy's story.

"What was he like?" she asked. "This dragonborn?"

"Everything he told my parents was a lie. I was little more than a glorified servant, cleaning his tower,
preparing his meals, polishing his talons, looking
after his birds and beasts, and worst of all . . . wip-
ing up the mess after his wretched experiments."

Here he winced, and Zelli sensed he was leaving out
certain details for her benefit. They passed the twin
sphynx statues standing sentinel outside the dean's
office. All was quiet. At the end of the hall, the lift to
the dormitories waited, still empty at that early hour.

"Morbide was always a nasty sort, but he changed

over the years. His experiments . . . I dare not tell you what I saw him do. It frightened me—shrieks and howls came from the dungeons of the tower, cries of suffering day and night. I had to leave. I had to." His amber eyes became glossy, but he blinked that away swiftly. "I stole one of his alchemical tomes, sure that I would soon be locked in those dungeons. I taught myself a bit of brewing and dropped a sleeping draft into his supper one night. He kept a few odd baubles and bits, so I took what I could carry and ran."

As they neared the dormitory lifts, Tavian touched the amulet around his neck, nestled beneath his striped scarf. "This amulet was one of the things I stole. I was wearing it around my neck when I was ambushed not far from the dragonborn's tower. They were dragons! Not just dragonborn, actual dragons." He laughed and pretended to faint back. His laugh was strained, and the memory must have been painful, Zelli mused. "I thought my doom was certain, but they did not attack. They took me for a dragon and raised me as their own. I didn't think the amulet's transformation would fool real dragons, but the magic is strong."

"That's amazing," Zelli breathed, admiring the

winking violet jewel set in gold around his neck. "And they have no idea you're a human?"

"No." He grinned, but it seemed sad to her. Forlorn. "Perhaps they have not been kind, but they have been so much better to me than Morbide. They can never find out; I could never survive without their protection. Even if they only tolerate me, in my heart I do feel like one of them, and wearing it makes me feel like I truly belong."

"Nobody knows?" she asked. "Not even your friends?"

Tavian pursed his lips. "No, I . . . nobody knows. There are no friends to discover my secret, for the others shun me for reasons I cannot understand. Only you know my secret. Please don't tell anyone, not a soul. I don't know what I'd do if they ever knew the truth. I need to keep walking this path; it's the only thing that makes me feel safe."

Zelli had been ready to spill all of it to the Danger Club the second she saw them again, but now she wasn't so sure. He looked so nervous, so tense, as if she might throw back her head and scream his secret to the world at any second. There was no reason for him to trust her right away, yet he had, and she wanted to prove worthy of that trust.

"I promise," she told him, meaning it. "Your secret's safe with me."

6

The ancient, tarnished lift gears began to tremble and scream, chains rattling as the platform lowered down toward them.

Two pairs of feet came into view—two tiny hook-clawed scaly things and big fluffy paws with carefully manicured talons. Snabla tossed his fists into the air, hurling himself off the lift before it stuttered to a stop. An oversized Flumphs jersey trailed along the stones behind him as he kicked and punched, humming an out-of-tune rendition of the school fight song.

"Firssst match of the Tourney today!" he whooped.

"Good morning, Zelli," Hugo greeted her. Bauble was there, too, of course, tucked safely into the big leather pack on Hugo's back. Given the rustling and panting behind Hugo, Flash was somewhere deeper in the bag. "You are up rather early." He then noticed the dragon beside her and gasped. "Oh! Who is this?"

"Yes! Introductions if you please, Zelli," Bauble piped up, elated.

Snabla's spinning and cheering came to an abrupt halt, and he squinted up at Tavian, tongue poking out in concentration.

"Snabla? Hugo? Bauble? This is Tavian. He's . . . a red dragon. I mean, obviously. Obviously he is a red dragon. We bumped into each other yesterday," Zelli said. "Tavian, this is everyone."

He smirked and inclined his head graciously as he had to her before. "Charmed, absolutely."

"Mind your p'sss and q'sss," Snabla lisp-hissed, poking a narrow claw at Tavian's chest. "I'm the only dragon in the Danger Club!"

"You are not a dragon," Bauble exasperatedly reminded him.

"My cousssin—"

"Isn't real," Bauble finished for him. Snabla nearly leapt out of his jersey with rage, but Bauble nimbly added, "And to my knowledge, Tavian is not a member of the Danger Club."

Snabla opened and closed his snout a few times, placated.

"Yet," Zelli heard Bauble murmur.

The kobold tiptoed

forward, agile, and gave a long sniff in the dragon's direction. He narrowed his eyes. "You don't sssmell right. Ssstrange."

Zelli cleared her throat and cut in. "I was just coming to find all of you. Tavian and I saw something that looked like a portal near the forest yesterday. That's how we met. He's heard rumors about our battle with the necromancer, isn't that amazing?"

Out of the corner of her eye, she noticed his brief, grateful look. She wouldn't tell his secret, not when he seemed so reliant on the amulet ruse to feel like himself. Zelli could relate, knowing how odd and frightening it was to feel like someone could discover your secret at any moment, and gobble you up the next. The Danger Club were different, but he didn't know them at all. She hoped, in time, he would come to feel as comfortable around them as she did. It was up to Tavian when he wanted to divulge his truth.

"And I told my mother about the door I found in the caves yesterday. She's going to talk to the dean about it, so even she thinks it's something important," Zelli continued, eager to be away from the thorny subject of Tavian's identity.

"A door?" Tavian asked, lifting a brow ridge. "How curious. . . ."

"How *extraordinary*!" Bauble exclaimed. "We really should examine that etching in the caves even

closer. Perhaps Hugo can take a sketch. The opening Tourney match won't start for at least another hour, so we may as well make good use of our time."

"Bauble is very efficient," Zelli explained. "They're a mimic. Other mimics can turn into almost anything, but Bauble struggles with becoming dangerous items."

"Totally normal," Bauble added lightly. "I'll grow out of it."

"And Snabla here inherited an enchanted shield; he's incredibly brave. Hugo doesn't eat meat, which is unusual for owlbears, but he knows all there is to know about plants and herbs and potions." Zelli pointed to his bag as the owlbear shrugged. "And there's a blink dog called Flash in there somewhere. She will probably try to lick you. A lot."

"What a truly varied and merry crew," Tavian remarked. "It's an honor to meet those who defeated the necromancer at the Battle of Horntree Cavern. What's all this about a door in the caves?"

Zelli pivoted to walk back the way they came. She launched into the whole story for Tavian's benefit, telling him about their adventure to Horntree Village to track down missing schoolmates, their encounter with wolves in the forest that brought them Flash, and the harrowing descent into the necromancer's cave, where they met Zelli's real mother, Allidora Steelstrike, and stopped Lord Carrion from stealing

villagers and students alike. Tavian listened eagerly, and even seemed legitimately impressed by the time Zelli got to the part where they tied up the necromancer and Snabla left a sign reading "STINKY" around his neck.

"He kept threatening that more of his kind were coming," Zelli finished. By that point, they had backtracked all the way to the grotesquely carved, looming arches that led to the spiral staircase and the dungeons, pits, and caves below. "I can't shake the feeling that we're still in danger, and next time it will be worse. They're keeping Lord Carrion prisoner in the school, and he was sending us all bad dreams until I had a talk with him. He mentioned something about a secret hidden in the mountain, so I did my own research and it led me to that door in the caves."

"How resourceful you are," Tavian replied, nodding along sagely. "Dragons are wrong about you monsters—you really can be cunning and clever."

"Really?" Zelli squawked. "You don't think I'm being silly?"

"I think you're being rather rational," the dragon boy said. "I should like to see this door, in fact. It sounds fascinating."

"Sssnabla always believe Zelli! Sssnabla take her ssseriously, too!" the kobold cried, racing ahead. He jumped, grunting, scratching at the wall until he could

reach a black metal ring, then snatched the torch out of it. "Thisss way! Thisss way to ugly crawly cavesss!"

"I wish more students at my school were willing to embark on these kinds of adventures," Tavian laughed, falling into step beside Hugo and Zelli as they started down the dark, winding path to the dungeons. Snabla had gone ahead, of course, determined to show off.

"What do you mean?" Bauble asked. Zelli could tell the mimic was bursting at the binding to pelt Tavian with a thousand questions. She was surprised Bauble managed to keep the impulse under control, as Zelli could see Bauble's bright bookish eyes practically counting every scale on Tavian's head. "Are dragons not inquisitive?"

"They are," the dragon replied. "But when you have wings and razor-sharp claws, when you can breathe fire or make great clouds of acid or ice, not much frightens you. Everyone at my school is so obsessed with their treasures and their jewels, they would think a mystery like this beneath them."

Zelli grinned at him crookedly. "It sounds nice to not really have any problems."

"Nice," Tavian agreed. "And boring."

"That could make one awfully complacent," Hugo pointed out wisely. "I think sometimes it is good to go on adventures and be afraid. I know I learned so much on our travels, and it made me a better owlbear."

"Sssnabla not afraid!" the kobold shouted over his bony shoulder, just a distant puddle of light vanishing down the stairs. "Sssnabla face any danger! Sssnabla hasss mighty shield and roaring dragon'sss blood!"

"That's our Snabla," said Zelli under her breath.

With nothing but a long, cold, fetid path ahead of them, it was time for Bauble to lob their never-ending list of questions at Tavian. He politely played along, so much so that Zelli couldn't help but glance at him sideways. In the field, he and the other dragons had been rude and standoffish. What changed? Was it because they were both humans, or something else?

Maybe like her, he, too, yearned to belong. According to Tavian, the other dragons were awful to be around. Maybe he felt as lonely and outcast as Zelli did sometimes. Kifin and Iasme Stormclash loved her unconditionally, but Zelli knew that would never be true of her classmates. It wasn't until she'd found the Danger Club that she'd felt truly accepted by monsters outside her family. Maybe Tavian needed a Danger Club of his own, but he wouldn't be with them long. Soon he would be expected to return to his kind. . . .

"Should we really be down here?" Hugo asked, a shake creeping into his voice as they descended from regular, disgusting dungeons to even dingier, colder, more disgusting caves. "It *is* forbidden."

"No," Zelli told him with a shrug. "But we already

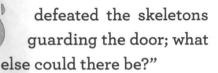

defeated the skeletons guarding the door; what else could there be?"

"Hexes? Ghosts? A l-lich?" Hugo stammered. "Just to name a few possibilities."

"We're together this time," Zelli reminded him, touching his elbow. "The Danger Club can tackle anything."

She led them deeper into the caves, puffs of their breath appearing by the light of Snabla's torch. It was far easier to find this time, as someone had gone to the trouble of lighting several more torches and placing them around the door itself. Shattered bones still littered the ground, but the design etched into the cave wall looked different now.

"It's like someone . . . polished it," Hugo observed.

"Ssstrange," Snabla whispered, scrunching his snout.

"Take me closer, Hugo," Bauble requested. The owlbear turned, backing up toward the wall so the mimic could get a better angle. "Doesn't it look just like a mirror?"

"It does," Zelli agreed.

"But the reflection isn't right," Tavian observed.

"Should we not see ourselves there?"

The oval within the gems and etched design did indeed glow and shimmer like a mirror, but what lay beyond was not a simple reflection. A whole world unfolded within it, hallways and zigzagging stairs, classrooms and vaulted libraries overflowing with books, corridors that seemed to go on for an eternity, with monsters and dragons milling together, talking and smiling as they went about their business.

"A school!" Bauble cried. They rocked toward the wall, throwing Hugo off balance, sending them both toward the strange, yellowed world beyond the mirror.

"No!" Zelli cried. "Don't touch it!"

She threw herself forward to catch Hugo, but the owlbear was too heavy. He toppled toward the mirror, arms out, eyes wide, Bauble soaring out of his bag and toward the mirrored door.

The instant Bauble touched the wall, the mirror image rippled outward, a deafening shock wave blowing the mimic in an arc over their heads. The mimic spun away into the darkness, emitting a high-pitched "Eeeeeeeee!" as they flew.

"Bauble!" Hugo gasped, picking himself up off the ground. Snabla was just a blur of ears and fire as he found the torch and waded through the fallen bones toward the back of the cave. They found their poor friend under a heap of rat fur, cobwebs, and several substances Zelli did not want to consider too carefully.

"I'm . . . I'm here!"

They dug through the debris toward the tiny voice, at last locating the mimic and pulling them free, Hugo using the end of his red-and-gold Flumphs scarf to wipe a smear of greasy something off Bauble, who, to cushion their fall, had transformed into a fluffy pillow.

"How intriguing! I have so much research to do!" the mimic laughed, eyes a bit dazed as they focused in the torchlight. Safe again, Bauble returned to their book form with a *pop!*

"I knew it," Hugo muttered. "This place is dangerous. We should not come down here again."

"Your friend is unharmed," Tavian Truescale pointed out. He made a face, moving farther away from the disgusting pile where they had located Bauble. "In need of a bath, no doubt, but unharmed. Did you not name yourselves the Danger Club?"

"You don't know the firssst thing about it!" Snabla snapped up into the dragon's face.

Hugo grumbled. "I just think—"

But Tavian had obviously had enough of the kobold's sour attitude, taking a step toward Snabla and looming over him. Zelli froze, knowing Snabla's temper could be legendary. *Would* be legendary.

"What I do know is that *you* are no dragon, little beast. If there is a secret to be found behind that door, we should press on. Or are you all as complacent as my fellow dragons?"

"Beassst? Beassst!" Snabla recoiled from Tavian, shriveling up like an ooze left too long in the sun. The kobold balled up his fists and danced to and fro, then punched one hand forward, threatening to strike. Tavian was far too quick for him, firing a thin stream of flame from his snout. It roasted a pile of rubbish next to Snabla harmlessly, but it was enough to make the little fellow shriek in surprise. Snabla's eyes bugged, and he shoved the torch toward Zelli, who fumbled to catch it without lighting herself on fire. Then the kobold stormed away, kicking bone bits and pebbles and rat carcasses as he went.

"Unlike ssstinky Tavian, Sssnabla can already sssee in the dark! Ha!"

The other monsters

and Tavian would gain their darkvision eventually, but Snabla's had come in early, in part due to his species' regrettably short lifespan. Zelli waved the torch in front of Tavian's face, jutting out her chin. She couldn't believe that Tavian, of all people—dragon people—was taunting someone for their heritage. "Was that really necessary? You could have burned him!"

"That was foolish," the dragon muttered. "I apologize. I . . . I don't usually take the bait like that."

Hugo had already cleaned off most of Bauble's cover and begun hurrying back toward the safety of the stairs and the upper dungeons. Hefting the torch above her head, Zelli urged Tavian to follow along.

"You talk to your friends that way?" she asked softly.

"No" was his curt reply. Then quieter, "I have no friends to insult."

"We'll go after him," Zelli called to Hugo, softening. "Don't worry."

And so they did, though with Snabla's churning little legs and ability to see flawlessly in the dark, he had quite the head start. It made Zelli sad to think that the kobold had grabbed that torch for them knowing they couldn't see the way he could.

"He has a good heart," Zelli blurted as they reached the dungeons above the cave. "He hasn't had the easiest time. His father is powerful, and Snabla struggles

to live up to that name. He tries his best, but it's a lot to put on one kobold."

"I regret my words even more," Tavian replied quietly. "I have always tried so hard to live up to the expectations of dragonkind, perhaps it has made me cold."

"I know red dragons are supposed to be vicious," said Zelli, snuffing out the torch and shoving it behind the strap holding her sword. "But you can be whatever kind of dragon you want to be."

Tavian ducked his head, and she wondered if that was the equivalent of dragon's blushing.

"He left tracks," Hugo pointed out, noticing a pattern of tiny black marks, small dirty footprints leading up out of the dungeons and toward the main corridor. "I have a feeling he returned to the festivities, yes? He should be easy enough to find."

Zelli wasn't so sure. His tracks would be useless once they reached the outdoors, and finding one tiny kobold in a sea of monsters and dragons sounded worse than needle-in-a-haystack odds. But they persevered, following the scuffed, dusty trail from the dungeon stairs to the hall, then right. Strangely, it seemed as if he had chosen to return to the dormitories instead of joining the other students outside at the Tourney. A trickle of monsters now ran through the halls, every single one of them dressed in bright red and gold.

Plenty of dark stares and whispers followed in Tavian's wake.

When they reached the dean's office, Zelli noticed it was no longer so sedate.

"Wait," she said, gathering Hugo close. Flash, who had gone quiet in the owlbear's bag, popped out to say hello, flicking her slimy tongue up the side of Zelli's face as Hugo neared. Bauble frowned, but then heard the same thing she had. "They're arguing," Zelli whispered. "Come here, behind this statue."

She had eavesdropped on the dean before in this very spot, and handily, it worked again. The other students flowing by paid no attention, too entranced by the promise of smoked fire toads, dipped spiders, ooze cheerleaders, and bloodthirsty competition.

"That's our dean," Tavian whispered, ears pinned back in alarm. "Cedaver."

"She looks much smaller," Zelli replied. The massive black dragon she had spotted in the clearing was now hardly larger than Tavian. Dean Cedaver still had the same arresting silvery eyes and elaborately curled horns, but she was far less intimidating at this size.

"It's a spell," Bauble explained, and Tavian nodded swiftly. "She wouldn't fit inside the school otherwise, but a dragon that ancient will know all sorts of magic."

Their own dean, the beholder Zxaticus, was in the middle of float-pacing before the black dragon. His

many eyes on their wiggly stalks slid back and forth erratically, but not enough to notice the door was cracked open. "Perhaps I should have anticipated this. Still, I do not appreciate you commandeering our only groundskeepers for the construction of your tent fortress. We offered spacious accommodations, but I suppose our dormitories are not grand enough for you," he was saying, and not courteously.

"They are not," the dragon agreed coolly. Even Cedaver's voice was mesmerizing: forceful, but muted enough that Zelli had to really train her ear to pick out every word. "My staff and students have brought adequate accommodations. Your groundskeepers were happy enough to comply. Honestly, Zxaticus, we cannot be expected to sleep in squalor."

"Squalor!" The beholder's eyes went rigid as he reared back. "Another insult!"

"What is insulting is that we ever trusted your deficient kind with the Nexus—"

A sustained, high howl interrupted the dragon. It

came from not far down the corridor, and by the time the Danger Club and Tavian tumbled out from behind the statue and ran, a group had gathered.

Gathered around Snabla.

The kobold lay on his back, deathly still, his scream already silenced as he stared with big, unblinking eyes up at the ceiling, his hands curled into tight claws. A further commotion followed as the professors and deans emptied out from the offices, joining the students circled around Snabla.

"Little thing is dead, I think," muttered a red gelatinous cube. Apparently satisfied, it slid away down the hall toward the outer doors.

"No, look! It's moving!" another student cried.

"Snabla!" Zelli and Hugo went to kneel beside their friend. If he had been grievously injured, Zelli didn't notice any signs. Flash appeared at the kobold's side, licking his pointed face desperately. "Snabla? Can you hear us?"

"Sssneaky!" Snabla croaked, one eyelid finally rising and lowering. Zelli covered her face, relieved. "Ssstinky, sssneaky Carrion poking around in hall!"

Zelli couldn't have heard him right. Carrion? As in Lord Carrion?

"Be gone from here!" Zxaticus bellowed. "Summon Noggin and Needler! We have an injured student here! Disperse! Disperse! I shall send you all to see

Nihildris! Disperse!"

Zelli, Tavian, and Hugo—carrying Bauble and Flash—backed away reluctantly. The other students quickly lost interest. The fate of one undersized kobold did not rate next to the temptations of the Tourney. Still, the Danger Club remained, looking on as Professor Cantrip oozed forward, his face upside down. He was an alchemist stuck inside the jiggling emerald cube forever, and apparently the most qualified to inspect Snabla. The dragon dean looked on, slightly apart.

"Sssneaky thief ssskulking in hall! I sssay: no! You our prisssoner! I attack! I sssurprise! But Carrion too quick for Sssnabla, ssstrike with chain!" Snabla breathed deeply, then propped himself up. He winced as soon as he tried to stand and collapsed back to the ground. A visible red slash mark split the scales on his forehead.

"What did this thief look like? Did you recognize them?" Professor Cantrip asked. He had long ago lost his flesh, just a half-digested skeleton inside the cube, and his voice emerged watery and distant from within the depths of the gel.

"Sssnabla recognize Carrion'sss purple robe! He essscape! Essscape to torment ssstudentsss and Sssnabla in particular!"

Zelli stood just far enough away from Snabla to

notice Cedaver and Zxaticus exchanging a troubled glance. She clutched Hugo's wrist. Was it possible?

"We can take him to the healer," Zelli volunteered. She wanted to hear more from Snabla, and she was sure the professors would shoo them away if she didn't speak up and make herself useful quickly. "We're Snabla's friends. He will feel more comfortable if we go along. Hugo can carry him."

Hugo, despite already carrying both Bauble and Flash, nodded eagerly.

"Very well," Zxaticus sighed. "If Lord Carrion has truly escaped, then we must investigate at once. But do not be trouble for Noggin and Needler. Leave that poor kobold to heal, do you understand me?"

"Of course! No trouble at all, sir!" Bauble chirped, too keen. The beholder looked twice at Bauble, apparently noticing that the normally fastidious mimic was covered in unspeakable filth.

"Now, Hugo, before they change their minds," Zelli muttered, elbowing the owlbear along. Hugo snapped into action, lumbering over to Snabla and scooping him up with ease, as if he were no more than a dead leaf. As she and Hugo turned to go, Tavian marched up right alongside them. Zelli hadn't expected that.

"Quickly!" Zxaticus was saying, leading the other

professors away. "With me!"

Neither had Cedaver, sweeping in front of them and fixing Tavian with a withering glare.

"I expected more from a vaunted student like you, Truescale," the dean scolded. "You know better than to associate with these . . . dungeon dwellers." She made her own way down the corridor, just a few steps, but in the direction of the outer doors. "Come, now. Leave these monsters; they can tend to their friend well enough."

"As you say," Tavian replied, bowing his head, wilting. He seemed strange, shy, not even sparing a glance in Zelli's direction. But then, he had to go with his kind. He wasn't a monster like them. This had all happened because he'd lashed out at Snabla. The kobold would have never run off alone if Tavian hadn't insulted him so cruelly. Tavian walked the path of the dragon, and that meant there was no place for him among dirty, deficient dungeon dwellers like the Danger Club.

"Go," Zelli told him to his back. "We can take care of our friend."

7

Noggin and Needler's yawning cabinet of curiosities lay tucked in the labyrinthine administration wing beside the forebodingly long corridor leading to the refuse trench, where the academy's garbage went to be burned by leaping, burning, flaming fire elementals. This wing was generally to be avoided—nobody, not even the toughest monsters, wanted to end up at Noggin and Needler's hovel, smell the garbage trench, or get dragged to the mind flayer counselor's office.

While Snabla lay clutching his head, moaning, and wheezing on a straw-stuffed cot in the corner, Zelli, Hugo, and Bauble waited across the room, trying not to disturb any of the thousands of strange concoctions packed onto the iron shelves bolted to the wall. A single stray elbow could cause a catastrophe. Several cages of toads, small birds, and snails hung above the ettin's overstuffed desk. A strong odor of alcohol and

astringent couldn't completely cover up the more pro-
nounced reek of mildew.

The ettin stood just over ten feet tall, with two heads
sprouting from its sloped shoulders. One head, Noggin's, was clean-shaven, a pair of red-tinted spectacles
pinching his bulbous nose and his mouse-brown hair
combed neatly to one side. The other head, Needler's,
wore a shaggy beard studded with all manner of oddi-
ties—bird's feet, iron rings, wooden beads, and bits of
forgotten breakfast.

"Be a dear and fetch me that cobalt vial on the shelf behind you, young lady," the Noggin head asked kindly.

Zelli began to search in something of a panic. *Which blue vial?* There were about sixteen different glass containers filled with bluish liquid. She picked a darker one and offered it to Noggin while the Needler head gave her a wild stare, one blue eye twitching.

"No! No! Cobalt! I said cobalt!" Needler shouted, showing her a pair of sharp, fang-like tusks.

"Patience, Needler, let her try again!" Noggin chided.

"Try the one with the green cork," Bauble suggested in a whisper. The mimic couldn't be of much use handling vials, but their sharp mind and expansive base of knowledge always helped. "Seems to me like a Bind

Wound potion. It's probably what he needs."

Zelli thanked the mimic under her breath and fetched the green-corked bottle, which Needler ripped out of her hand without another word but all sorts of indecipherable muttering.

The ettin doused a rag in the cobalt-colored mixture and hovered it over Snabla. The kobold rolled back and forth on the cot, clutching his chest.

"Sir? Sirs?" Zelli ventured softly. Hugo turned to regard her with his head tilted in curiosity. She pursed her lips in response and shrugged as if to say: *It's worth a try.*

"Yes, child?" Noggin murmured, keeping his back to her.

"Do you have any idea why Dean Zxaticus and Dean Cedaver don't like each other?"

A trilling laugh ripped out of Noggin's throat, loud and strange enough that Snabla's eyes snapped open. Then he seemed to remember his injury and performance and gradually closed them again.

"Oh, girl, there's more history there than all the scrolls and tomes in the libraries of all the world." The ettin sniggered. Oh? Bauble and Hugo perked up at that. Interesting. "But your friend here was only grazed by a withering touch and slashed a bit by a chain. I shall set him to rights now. Yes. Yes. . . . Hold still, Snabla, and whatever you do, do not sneeze."

Snabla's nose immediately began to twitch.

"NO RUDDING SNEEZING!" Needler thundered.

Noggin sighed, grumbled some more, and returned to his desk, fetching a gnarled old staff. Streamers of bark peeled from the staff, though the top of it seemed alive with bright new growth and an infestation of flies. Snabla clutched his pointed nose with both hands, stuffing back a sneeze as the ettin returned and began waving the staff over the kobold's shoulder and chanting.

"What do you suppose happened?" Zelli whispered while the healer was distracted.

"Your dragon pal was awfully rude," Bauble pointed out. "Maybe Zxaticus thinks all dragons are too proud."

"True," Hugo agreed, nodding, and keeping one eye on Snabla's condition. Flash had already fallen asleep in his bag, snoring deeply. "Dean Cedaver did not seem happy about him spending time with us. Even with a rivalry between the schools, it felt harsh. . . ."

"*Blast.*" Zelli closed her eyes tightly. "This is just another distraction! Zxaticus is never going to take us seriously, not if he's spending all his time arguing with Dean Cedaver."

"And don't forget the Tourney," said Bauble, despondent. "I can't believe *I* almost forgot about the Tourney."

"If Lord Carrion really escaped, they might blame me for it. I was the last person to see him," Zelli whispered, coming to the realization with a pit forming in her stomach. If they found traces of the spiders she had thrown on him, then they might start asking questions, and the slaad who'd gifted them to her might come forward. . . .

She ducked her face into her hands.

"A bunch of tickling spiders couldn't have freed him," Bauble replied softly, carefully. "There has to be another explanation."

"Or perhaps Snabla was mistaken," Hugo said. "He was in a rather agitated state; he might have only thought he saw Lord Carrion. . . ."

"This is all a mess," Zelli sighed. "Someone is using the cover of the Tourney to cause all this chaos."

"And it seems to be working," Hugo agreed.

Noggin yanked his fly-infested staff away from Snabla just as the kobold unleashed a ferocious sneeze, one that sent him rolling off the cot.

"Eh." The ettin hobbled away. "He will be fine. Rest! Yes. Yes . . . He must rest." Noggin and Needler spun around, their four eyes settling on Zelli. Noggin pointed the end of his staff at her and glared. "And you! All of you! Keep your heads on a swivel, eh? Eh. Yes. Careful now, careful. I don't like this. Don't like it down to my bones. A withering touch is not often

seen. Not often. . . ." Spitting on the ground and narrowly missing Snabla, the ettin returned to his desk, hunting around for something under the mountains of parchment and discarded potion bottles. "Zxaticus must know. Eh, yes. Yes, he must know. . . ."

"You want I should stick the kobold with some needles?" Needler offered.

"What? No. No! Preposterous. Be silent, Needler. Let me concentrate, eh! The dean must know of this."

Hugo stuffed Bauble back into his bag on top of Flash and hurried over to Snabla, who lay on the ground, still recovering from his sneeze and treatment.

"Know what?" Zelli asked, lingering behind the ettin.

"Eh? What? No! Shoo! Shoo, now. This will not concern you. . . ." Noggin returned to his search, discovered an old stub of charcoal, and began scribbling. Needler fixed her with an angry glare, his hand twitching to reach for something sharp and poky. While Hugo helped Snabla toward the door, Zelli hazarded one last glance, peeking over the ettin's knurled forearm. His handwriting seemed more like lost, ancient runes discovered in a delve, but she managed to decipher a single word: *scholarship*.

Hugo's big hand closed around her upper arm, dragging her away from the mumbly, rumbly goblin.

The gargantuan iron door swung shut with a bang, sending a cascade of bats diving overhead.

"Sssnabla walk on hisss own," the kobold declared, pushing away from Hugo and the owlbear's helping hand. "Brave! Sssnabla sssurvive Lord Carrion alone! Bravessst now of all kobold!"

"What a relief that you weren't seriously hurt," Bauble called down from Hugo's bag. Snabla set forth on his own, weaving across the stone floor on unsteady, teetering feet. "Was it really Lord Carrion?"

"Of course it wasss! Sssnabla prove!"

"Snabla . . . ," Zelli cautioned. "Snabla, wait!"

The kobold ignored her, winding his way back toward the main corridor. "No! Sssnabla no afraid. Return to ssscene of crime! Find sssneaky dirty necromancer who messs with Sssnabla!"

It wasn't even noon yet and Zelli craved a nap; she was ready to collapse from exhaustion. But she caught up to Snabla, digging for a second wind, and took the kobold by the shoulder, forcing him to stop.

"If this is about what that dragon said to you . . ."

"Who? Not familiar with any ssstupid dragon!" Snabla took a swing at the air, spun, and fell on his rump. Zelli hooked her wrists under his arms and scooped him back onto his feet.

"But your cousin—" Bauble began.

"Leave Sssnarlathat out of thisss!"

"But Noggin told you to rest!" Bauble shimmied over the edge of Hugo's bag, giving Snabla their most grimly determined frown. Snabla didn't seem to notice.

"No ressst! No need it!" He was going to run straight into a wall if one of them didn't intervene.

Hugo shrugged helplessly at Zelli. Slowly, the owlbear said, "The professors will take care of Lord Carrion if he escaped. There is little we can do about it unless they request our help. What . . . about . . . the Tourney?"

That brought Snabla's teetering and tottering to an abrupt halt. He twisted in place, droopy eyes suddenly ablaze with inspiration. Zelli winced. *Oh no.*

"Tourney! Tourney! Tourney! Tourney!"

Zelli pressed her fingers against her temples. Unbelievable. But then maybe it was totally believable—of all of them, Snabla had been the most excited for the Tourney of Terror, and now, thanks to Zelli's hunt for necromantic clues, he was missing out on most of it. She took a deep breath and told herself she was doing the right thing for her friend. With his baggy, dirtied tunic dragging on the stones behind him, Snabla weaved his way toward the tall arches at the opposite end of the corridor. The school lay quiet and abandoned again, so much so that Zelli couldn't help but glance over her shoulder as they followed

Snabla, unable to escape the sense that someone was watching them.

"What do you know about withering touches?" Zelli asked Bauble as they kept an eye on their recuperating kobold companion. Bobbing along on Hugo's back, the mimic pursed their lips.

"Nothing good," Bauble sighed. "Undead magic. Nothing a professor here would teach, and nothing a student here should know. It might really have been Lord Carrion."

"What do you want to wager something evil came through that portal I saw near the trees and freed the necromancer?" Zelli wondered aloud.

"I have a bad feeling about this," Bauble replied, grim.

"Me too," Hugo chimed in.

"Me three," said Zelli. "Snabla would, too, if he had anything but Goreball on the mind."

"We have to be gentle with him," Bauble told her. "He's suffered a terrible fright. I can understand why he would prefer to be distracted right now."

Distracted. Zelli hunched, bottling up her frustration. Everyone was distracted! The professors, the students, Snabla, her own mother . . .

"Look on the bright side," Bauble added, just as they reached the end of the emptied corridor and passed below the arches. "If there's a necromancer skulking

around the school, he'll have to deal with dragons, too, not just monsters. Lord Carrion won't get far with all of the staff from two schools searching for him."

Zelli hadn't considered that. The thought soothed her, but only temporarily. Carrion had seemed too crazed and determined when she visited him; she couldn't imagine him easily giving up his crusade for the so-called Lord of Death. Outside, the grounds were abuzz with activity. The soaring tent roosts built by the cyclops groundskeepers loomed above the dozens and dozens of canvas-and-wood structures running along the right side of the Goreball field. The stands were filled to overflowing, two separate sections, one for each team, flashing with colored streamers, scarves, and pennants. The flumphs and dragons waited for the first match to begin, congregating on their home halves and performing tricks and displays to intimidate the other team. Two nimble green dragons performed loops, just skimming the grass with their claws on each daring descent toward the ground. The gibbering mouther undulated in its cage at center field, ready to be unleashed. Zelli spotted her ooze roommate on the sidelines with the other cheerleaders, red-and-gold felt pompoms stuck to her jiggling green mass.

Golden confetti-like coins drifted through the air. Zelli caught one bit of gilt parchment with her hand,

and found Dean Cedaver's face on one side of the confetti coin. A few fire elementals and Mavis, the dining chamber overseer, stoked a bonfire high on the near side of the pitch, closest to the school, handing every passing student a bowl of steaming plovers' eggs or a goat haunch on a skewer. Over near the Waterdeep Dragons' tent city, Zelli could just make out a few older red dragons running their own dragon tailgate.

Horns blasted; spur-of-the-moment cheers erupted; a pair of blue dragons flew a banner overhead reading 1000 YEARS OF VICTORY; roasty, sugary, briny, savory smells perfumed the breeze; banners snapped; pride blazed and hopes bubbled to boiling.

It overwhelmed the senses.

Zelli almost didn't notice a trio of red dragons approaching. She did when, gazing around at everything to smell, hear, and behold, she ran right into Snabla's back. The kobold froze, glaring at the dragons. She recognized Tavian, of course, and he was accompanied by the other two she'd had the unfortunate pleasure to meet near the vanishing portal. Tavian detached and trotted over to them, Snabla's hackles rising by degrees as he approached.

"Hello again," Tavian said, a little hoarse. "I just wanted to, well . . ."

"Ssspit it out!" Snabla raised one little fist.

"Apologize, actually. I owe you an apology, Snabla.

I was completely out of line to question you in the caves, and I am most sorry."

Over Tavian's shoulder, the two red dragons rolled their eyes, the boy calling, "Are you finished? Their stench will get all over you!"

"I apologize for Varika and Bowen, too. They are always impatient, and they always speak their minds," Tavian said softly.

Hugo snorted. "I'll say."

"Apology accsssepted," Snabla hissed, sticking his pointed nose in the air with a sniff. "For now."

Then the kobold swiveled on one wobbly foot, chin still pointed to the sky, and went about sampling all the Tourney of Terror had to offer.

Zelli could only remember being so exhausted the evening they returned from the necromancer's cave outside Horntree Village. She didn't know a person could be exhausted down to the roots of their hair. When at last the first match of the Tourney was over (a narrow defeat for the flumphs, the dragons scoring thirteen to their eleven), she slumped back to the dormitories, bidding her friends good night before shouldering open the door to her room.

Only after she crossed to her own side of the

chamber did she realize the door had come open too easily. Unlocked. But her roommate wasn't there, and Zelli was always very careful about locking up their belongings. A thin shaft of moonlight pierced the window, illuminating a mess of tunics and trousers spilling from the trunk at the foot of her bed.

Quite suddenly, Zelli was fully awake and in a panic. She rushed to the tossed clothes, finding that someone had gone digging through her things. Fear tightened her throat as she searched and searched, terrified that someone had stolen the one thing that marked her as human and linked Zelli to her birth mother.

"No, no, no, no . . . ," she whispered. "It has to be here. It can't be gone. . . ."

Zelli was a girl of few possessions, and it did not take her long to reach the bottom of the recklessly sorted pile. Under a crumpled knit boot sock, she found it, and she sat back on her heels, clutching the little Steelstrike medallion to her chest. Allidora

Steelstrike had given it to her when they met with the promise that it could summon her, if ever Zelli was in danger and needed the human adventurer's help. Zelli didn't know if she ever intended to use it, but the thought of losing the one thread tying her to her birth mother was unbearable.

Climbing to her feet, Zelli tried to mentally catalog her belongings, searching for what might be out of place. Other than the obvious mess, she couldn't decide if there was anything missing. She didn't own anything valuable besides the medallion.

Zelli kicked numbly at a pair of trousers, too tired to clean up the mess, and too disquieted to climb into bed and sleep. Lord Carrion had likely escaped, and what if he had come looking for her? Or something of hers? His creepy voice slithered through her mind. *Her arrival is inexorable, but you can hasten it along, girl.*

Hasten it along how? *What did he come looking for?* she wondered. And then: *Did he find it?*

8

Early the following morning, Zelli stood shoulder to shoulder with two bleary-eyed bugbears as they stood outside the school, mist swirling at their feet. Dean Zxaticus positioned his round, floating bulk in front of the doors leading into the main corridor. Flanked by Professor Cantrip, Professor Gast, Impro Vice, Noggin, Needler, Shinka Bookbinder, and Nihildris the mind flayer, the beholder used his boomingest voice to inform the gathered, shivering students that access to the school would be limited for the rest of the day.

"It's been brought to my attention," Dean Zxaticus told them, "that several rooms in the dormitories were entered without permission. Until the culprit is apprehended, we must take all possible precautions. If you need any items from your room, please speak to Durg, Gageth, or Ergakk and they will assist you. If you see

anything suspicious, alert a professor immediately. Thank you."

Gageth and Ergakk, the cyclops groundskeepers, waited off to the side. Durg, presumably, was still doing a poor job guarding the now-empty Hall of Eternal Suffering & Monotony.

"All meals will be served outdoors," Zxaticus finished, "and Tourney of Terror activities will proceed as scheduled."

"Of course they will," Zelli muttered bitterly. If the thief sneaking around the school was important enough to close off the mountain, then it was important enough to stall the festivities, too. "Not a word about Lord Carrion."

The bugbear hunkered down under a blanket next to Zelli glared. "Party pooper."

Zelli ignored them, watching a low, dark, blurry item emerge from the archway and doors behind Zxaticus. It was brownish in color, and rolled at dizzying speed, disappearing into the milling, muttering, whispering crowd of monsters. When the professors turned and retreated into the school to begin their search, the object veered toward Zelli, swerving around goblins, oozes, slaadi, and gnolls until it came to a rolling stop at Zelli's feet.

The barrel bumped gently against her ankles; then, along one of the iron bands hugging the wooden slats, two eyes appeared, blinking.

"Bauble?" Zelli laughed. "What's with the new look?"

"Ugh. I hate it! These grass stains will be impossible to get out. . . ."

Hugo lumbered his way toward them, removing his spectacles to rub them on his woolly vest. He stifled a yawn as Bauble tipped themselves onto one edge. Snabla appeared not long after, an eye mask resting on his forehead.

"Grab the books in there," came Bauble's muted voice.

Zelli reached into the barrel and retrieved three solid tomes, each with soft leather covers and dense, uncut pages. All of them looked old and precious, and Zelli held on to them carefully while Bauble transformed back into their preferred bookish appearance.

"Here," Zelli said, offering Hugo the crocheted blanket from around her shoulders. "Help Bauble."

The owlbear gathered Bauble into the blanket, helping them warm up and dry off. The dewy grass had left the mimic a bit damp.

"Wait a minute," Zelli chuckled, holding up one of the books. "Did you sneak into the library for these?"

The mimic's eyes glittered. "I couldn't sleep at all last night! Not a wink! My mind was just spinning, spinning . . . Something Dean Cedaver said yesterday

kept bothering me, so I thought I would pop down to the library before they locked us out."

"Bauble take page from Sssnabla's book! Ssso intrepid!" Snabla beamed. The mark on his forehead seemed much better.

"Why thank you, Snabla. It was ingenious, if I do say so myself."

"These are all about keys and keystones," said Zelli, checking the titles Bauble had brought.

The mimic, cozily swathed in the blanket crocheted by Zelli's mother, nodded excitedly. "And that is not all! Take a glance at who wrote them."

"*The Great Unlockening*," Zelli read aloud, squinting at the bindings. "*Vanished and Banished: A History of Rare Artifacts*, and *The Barriers We Build: Unlocking the Weave*, by Cedaver the Circumlocutious." Her eyes widened. "The dragon dean wrote these?"

"Indeed, and if her name is anything to go by, they won't be light reading," Bauble sighed. "You know I love a dense paragraph, but this might be a bit much, even for me. Still! I heard her mention something called the Nexus Marker to Dean Zxaticus. We studied portal markers in History of Wretched Relics, so I thought it might be something similar."

"Good find," Zelli whispered, amazed. "We can start poring over these during breakfast!"

"No ssstinky ressssearch," Snabla whined, his

shoulders sagging. "Sssecond match today, plenty of time for flumphsss to ssscore pointsss!"

Side by side with Hugo, Bauble waited until Snabla was a few paces ahead of them to say, "We can do our stinky research while Snabla watches the Goreball drills. Win-win."

"Indeed. The only win-winning you monsters will be doing."

Zelli and Hugo (and therefore Bauble) turned to find Tavian had carved his way through the dispersing students. He looked so completely like a dragon—and acted like one, too—that Zelli sometimes had a hard time remembering he was a human under that disguise.

"Just a jest," Tavian added, though it would be hard to argue against him. The Dungeon Academy Flumphs' trophy chest was empty for a reason. "I'm trying it out. Joking. Such things do not usually go over so well with other dragons."

"What are you doing here?" Zelli asked. She had assumed he would stick with the students from his school that day after being chastised by the dean.

"I saw the crowd and wanted to see what all the commotion was about," the dragon replied. He glanced down. "Am I intruding?"

"Not at all," Zelli said, before Bauble or Hugo could respond. Then, sheepish, she glanced at her friends, and found that they were silent. And dumbfounded.

She couldn't exactly blurt out that Tavian was a human like her, and an outcast. "He did apologize to Snabla!"

"My behavior yesterday was totally inappropriate," Tavian added solemnly. "You have all extended such kindness to me, I hardly deserve it. Sometimes I can be as sharp as a thornslinger."

At that, Hugo brightened. "A fellow horticulturalist?"

Tavian was not, in fact, as versed in flora as Hugo the owlbear, but he could at least keep up with Hugo's running account of all the lovely plants he kept in his room. His request for an east-facing room had been granted that semester, and ever since, his bulbous violet had really been flourishing. He had even constructed a wooden box for his closet to raise daggerroot, and recently it had propagated, and wasn't that marvelous? Tavian agreed that it was. The temporary rift between Tavian and the Danger Club was forgotten, and he looked relieved to be in their good graces again, beaming at Hugo as they swapped plant facts. Hugo did most of the swapping, but Tavian seemed content to listen. Zelli was glad they were giving him a chance—he was the first human she had met of her own age, and she didn't want to give up on him yet. They were kindred spirits, both in disguise, only she had found monsters who accepted her, and Tavian deserved the same. It made her feel good knowing she

was changing his life for the better.

While most of the students congregated near the bonfire where Mavis had begun boiling cauldrons and roasting meat, the Danger Club and their dragon tagalong made their way to the prime front row of the Dungeon Academy stands. Ahead, Professor Storm-clash tried to rouse the sleepy Goreball team, leading them in stretches.

Snabla followed along, choosing to let Bauble and Zelli handle the research. After every side bend, he turned to glance furtively at Tavian, then narrowed his eyes and sniffed. Hugo pulled Bauble out of his pack and set them down on one of the long, sturdy wooden slats, giving the mimic a better vantage for study.

Zelli did not notice the broad shadow falling across them until it was too late, and her mother loomed, beaming down at them, her fur mussed from the wind and dewy air.

"There you are, Zellidora. Excited for the match? You certainly found good seats!"

Zelli artlessly fell across the books open on the stands, plastering on a crooked smile. "The match! Yes! Elated, um, naturally."

Professor Stormclash huffed. "I see. And those look like library books under your armpit. You wouldn't have broken the dean's decree and gone into the school today, would you?"

Bauble shrank.

"Are you seriously going to punish me for reading more?" Zelli bit back. Unbelievable. Was she supposed to apply herself and succeed at monster school or not?

"No, but I would punish you for breaking the rules."

Zelli did the one thing that was sure to make her mother's blood boil. She rolled her eyes. "But we're just having a study club. We're not even doing anything wrong!"

"There are rules for a reason, Zellidora, and they exist for your protection. The school grounds are dangerous right now! I wish you would listen to your teachers," Professor Stormclash told her, her voice the same cold steel as her daughter's.

"And I wish my teachers would listen!"

Zelli almost never raised her voice like that with her parents. She flinched, watching the minotaur go completely still, as if Zelli had lashed out with her hand instead of her words. But like a sudden spring thaw, Professor Stormclash gradually came back to

herself. Her gaze did not soften, and she put both fists on her hips. A hard breath ruffled the furry fringe falling over her eyes.

"We *are* listening. The school is being searched, Zellidora; you got your wish." A student called to her mother from the field, and the minotaur sighed and turned away. "Just . . . Just stay here, all right? Where I can see you. . . ."

The ground and stands trembled as her mother stormed away.

"I take it that's your mum?" Tavian murmured. Even he, a dragon, cowered.

"In the flesh," Zelli sighed.

"Hey!" Bauble nudged a book closer to Zelli until it bumped her knee. "Observe here, Zelli. While you were taking the fall for my library pilfering, I discovered something. Dean Cedaver has written extensively about this Nexus Marker. It's all rather dense, but I think I can make heads or tails or both of it by the end of the afternoon. Ah, but it would be so much better if we could be in the actual library—a pamphlet or two on keystones would help me decipher this faster. . . ."

"Not an option," Zelli replied. She stared across the students waiting for breakfast and toward the doors leading into the academy. The mind flayer Nihildris with their bruise-colored, many-tentacled face and ominously red cloak darkened the paving stones there,

eyes bouncing from student to student with ceaseless, alarming vigilance.

"Well. Then it will take time," Bauble explained.  "I'm only one genius."

"I can help!" Zelli protested, scooting one of the brick-heavy tomes onto her lap.

"Sure. Right!" Bauble muttered, eyes floating to the side. "Of course you can. Only—"

Zelli slammed her hand down onto the cover, displacing a cloud of ancient dust. "Only what?!"

"Only . . . your aptitude lies elsewhere, doesn't it? In swinging a sword, leading us into battle, bolstering spirits? There's nothing wrong with that, Zelli; we all have our interests." Bauble's features seemed to scatter across the cover, perhaps because Zelli had begun to tremble like a bubbling cauldron.

"I was the one who spoke to Carrion and found the door in the caves," Zelli replied through clenched teeth. Orcs, lurching vulture-beaked hook horrors, gnolls, owlbears, slaadi, and all manner of monsters had begun filling in the stands, clutching wooden bowls of slop. She lowered her voice, mindful of their fellow students. The Waterdeep Dragons had taken the field, flying loops as they waited for the starting whistle to blow.

"I'm not just a sword swinger," she added softly,

unclenching her fist on the cover of the book. For a moment, none of them spoke. Snabla grunted, wriggling his claws, struggling to touch his toes. A light breeze ruffled Bauble's pages. Flash popped out of Hugo's bag, sensed the tension, whined, and immediately disappeared again.

"You can never know what's really in someone's heart," Tavian said slowly. Zelli tried to meet his eye, for she knew deeply the truth of his words, but he avoided looking at her. "We all walk a road with our feet, the road others see, while traveling an invisible path in our dreams." He turned his narrow red head toward the Goreball pitch. "I was supposed to be out there flying with the team. They might lose because I sat out, but I could no longer say I was playing because I loved it, or because everyone depended on me." He closed his bright amber eyes, a strange half smile revealing a few fangs. "Sometimes I do not even . . . even . . ."

Know who I am, Zelli thought.

Tavian shook off that thought, blinking as if coming out of a deep slumber. "Only Varika and Bowen speak to me now, and one would be hard-pressed to call them friends."

"It doesn't matter what others expect," Hugo told the dragon. "Or what the dragons think of you. You have friends."

"That's right," Bauble added. "You have us. Snabla . . ." The mimic's eyes shifted toward the calisthenics-inclined kobold. "Snabla will come around."

The whistle blew. A cheer went up, a few globs of porridge flying as excited fists raised dirty spoons. And Tavian winced as, at once, the Dungeon Academy Flumphs went on the attack, pressing the gibbering mouther toward the dragon's goal line. Bauble returned to their research, prodding the book until Zelli had a clear view of the text, too. She grinned down at the mimic, who didn't seem to notice.

"Yesss! Firssst blood will be oursss!" Snabla shrieked, bouncing up and down on the grass. He had managed to shimmy his way into the line of ooze cheerleaders, and, Zelli could argue, he seemed as energetic as they did, if not more so. Maybe he needed to consider a new hobby.

Not only that, Snabla's estimation of the game seemed correct, too. The gibbering mouther neared the end of the dragons' half, the mist along the ground working in favor of the Flumphs. The fog obscured most of the monster players, making it difficult for the dragons to take control of the match.

"Were you really meant to be out there?" Hugo asked.

Tavian grinned, apparently pleased to be included once more. "I was. Do you know the game?"

"Know it? I live it." Hugo beamed out at the field, his taloned paws sandwiched between his knees as he sighed. "Well, as near as I can without actually playing." He stuck out his right leg and wiggled it. "Weak patella, you know."

"I had no idea," Zelli murmured. "I thought Snabla was the only Goreball fanatic."

"You see? Expectations will deceive you," Hugo chuckled. "Observe: the Flumphs have clustered on one side now as they attack; they must have determined the weak spot in the Waterdeep defense. This is a risky tactic, but it will be greatly successful if your mother has correctly identified a flaw."

"Really? You can tell all of that?" Zelli asked, astonished. "To me it just looks like a bunch of headless axe beaks running into each other."

Hugo and Tavian both shook their heads, exchanging amused smiles. On the field, one of the academy players shouted a spell, transforming into a beholder as large and imposing as Dean Zxaticus himself. The visiting dragon chasing them hesitated, stumbling backward, startled by the brief use of the polymorph spell.

"Your mother just deployed the Statue of Cyric maneuver," Tavian explained.

Zelli snorted. "The What of What?"

"Statue of Cyric," said Hugo. "It's a trick play made

famous by the Luskan Giants. A sudden deployment of the polymorph spell can confuse the other team, throw them into chaos for that play. You see, the game is intricate, a duel of the minds, of strategy, as well as a physical expression. . . ." Hugo indicated the field again, this time pointing to Professor Stormclash, and then the dragon's coach, a whip-thin green dragon with a snarling expression. "There are players on the Goreball field, but this is truly a game of Lanceboard controlled by your mother and the opposing overseer. Ah, but it is beautiful. Complex. One day I hope you learn to appreciate it, Zelli, but I am grateful to have a new friend who delights in it the way I do."

Tavian inclined his head. "I am humbled."

Zelli didn't have the heart to be jealous, and she did not have the time to learn all the many ins and outs of Goreball. The Nexus Marker demanded her attention instead. The Flumphs were having more success with the game than Zelli was with her research—Bauble was not lying when they said Cedaver's paragraphs on the Nexus felt indecipherable. To Zelli they were practically another language.

Astonishingly, my calculations suggest that only the kinetic potential created by three intersecting ley lines and rich, hidden diamond deposits would provide the necessary power for a barrier of such magnitude, a barrier encompassing the entire mountain. Yet this staggering confluence exists deep below Akhellon Ridge, providing a protective barrier that prevents certain magics and teleportation. Only a relic as powerful as the Nexus Marker could control such a shield; without it, the barrier could not persist.

Zelli pinched her nose, wondering if Bauble was absorbing a single word. The whistles, cheers, and general chaos of the clash demolished her concentration.

The bloodcurdling screams didn't help, either.

Zelli's head snapped up. *The bloodcurdling screams?* Tavian had stood up in the stands, his wings cocked and slightly back, one taloned hand pointing north.

"Does . . . Does your forest normally do that?" he whispered, stricken.

At first, Zelli thought a bizarre snowstorm had begun blowing onto the field sideways. Stranger things had happened. Dingy white shapes blasted out of the trees, driven as if they were fleeing for their lives. Some flew, some ran, some bounced, but they all had one thing in common. . . .

Bones. A thousand skeletons burst out of the Endless Forest—delicate, fragile bird skeletons and tiny hares, deer missing legs or heads, and stags with their white gleaming racks of antlers bobbing through the mist. Many of the skeletons were so strange or broken or unrecognizable that Zelli could only hazard a guess as to their origin—blocky-boned otyughs with spiny teeth spraying from their mouths and a galloping giant frog missing one back leg. Lightning-fast worgs smashed into each other as they fled the wood. An unholy noise rose from the treetops, the leaves rattling as all the undead creatures new and long buried in the earth erupted. Every mound, grave, and pit had seemingly emptied itself, hurling the skeletal contents at the school. Even across the field, Zelli heard branches deeper within snap and splinter, dislodging a flock of undead ravens

that raced toward the dragon tents and roosts, tearing through the canvas like a volley of arrows.

Porridge bowls flew as the monster students leapt to their feet, jelly, claws, and paws. Professor Stormclash gathered the flustered Goreball players to her, grabbing a wooden bench off the sidelines and snapping it in two, hefting one half as a shield, wielding the other as a club.

"Danger Club!" Zelli called, shucking her slippers and reaching for her practice sword. "You know what to do!"

"Sssnabla ready!" the kobold cried, scrambling back toward the stands to find his scaled shield. Flash scampered eagerly out of Hugo's bag, growling at the coming undead onslaught.

"What!" Bauble cried, transforming into a broadheaded shovel. "A strange!" Hugo grabbed Bauble by the handle, picking his way down the stand benches to join Zelli and Snabla. "Phenomenon!"

"Bauble! We can study it later!" Zelli called back breathlessly, whacking a skeletal worg to pieces as it lunged for her face. A clump of trees at the very edge of the wood split, cleaved by a gargantuan, twisting pillar of bone white. It thrust the smaller softwoods and saplings aside, jolting the ground with cumbersome, stumpy steps. "A treant!" Zelli shouted, holding her ground on bare feet. The living or, rather, *unliving*

tree creature slammed one twisted arm into the nearest pole holding up a dragon roost, collapsing the whole structure.

"Tavian? Are you with us?" asked Hugo over his shoulder, brandishing Bauble. "We could use your fire."

"I stand with you," Tavian Truescale declared. "A dragon side by side with the Danger Club!"

9

Every able and present professor, student, and dragon rushed the field. The Danger Club did not fight alone—Zelli's breath caught in her throat as she watched blue, green, white, black, and red wings flash as the Waterdeep Dragons lifted into the air.

"A dead tree?" Tavian called, his voice just rising above the terrible din of what had become a battlefield. "We will make quick work of them with my fire breath!"

"I wouldn't be so sure. . . ." Bauble trailed off, their flat shovel face smashing into a skeletal bird as Hugo deflected it. And just as the mimic predicted, many of the dragons were waylaid by the sudden storm of flying undead critters.

A silhouette appeared at the very edge of the forest, barely visible among the flattened trees and barrage of minions still exploding out of the woods. Their robes fluttered, floating along the fog

as if part of it. The figure raised their staff, and the bony birds circling the field began to gather, flying in unison, forming a growing vortex, a dizzying tornado of tiny, sharp bones. It moved across the Goreball pitch at the figure's command, and any dragon who flew near was knocked swiftly off course. Several treants emerged from the forest, each stepping over the robed figure before parting ways, one smashing the tents apart to the right of the field, another joining the first and lumbering with massive, quaking steps toward the school.

"We have to dismantle that vortex!" Bauble cried.

"But how?" Hugo asked, panting from using the mimic as a shield to smash incoming skeletons to pieces. Flash launched off of Hugo's shoulder yipping with excitement, vanishing into the fray to—once more—teleport among the smaller skeletons and pop them apart with a satisfying *crack!* This critter army far outnumbered what Zelli, Bauble, Hugo, Snabla, and Flash had faced in the necromancer's cave, and Zelli felt a wave of nauseating fear rise in her stomach. She swallowed it back—she had mastered her apprehension in the cave, and she would master this feeling, too. She had to, for as she looked around, she saw so many more familiar faces among the imperiled—her mother pushed toward the spinning storm of bones alongside her ooze roommate, Bloppy, the other cheerleaders,

Patty the bugbear and Gutrash the goblin, gnolls, elementals, and dao banding together against the undead.
Dean Cedaver rumbled along the sidelines, craning her
ebony head back before unleashing a thick, smog-like
cloud that dissolved bones instantly.

Any creature left standing seemed drawn in one
direction, Zelli noticed, the skeletal creatures fixat-
ing on the school. While treants wreaked havoc, the
remaining horde moved toward the academy and the
line of professors waiting at the entrance, the last line
of defense.

"Get me closer to that tornado," Bauble demanded.

"Azzz you command!" cried Snabla, hefting his
shield. "Dragon, help! Blow fire on ssshield!"

Tavian drew back, ducking and narrowly avoiding
a skeletal robin that zipped by like a spear.

"Trust what he says and do it," Zelli told him. "His
shield is magic!"

The red dragon shrugged and complied, inhal-
ing deeply before spitting a controlled stream of fire
against Snabla's rickety wooden shield. At once, its
edges began to glow crimson, then the enchantment
revealed itself, golden scales shining, piercing the
gloom of the day. Snabla led them, shield forward,
bashing every squirrel, hare, and badger that dared
too close. Zelli and Hugo followed, lashing out at any
critter who escaped Snabla's fury. Tavian took flight,

coasting just above their heads, breathing gouts of fire at any airborne enemies in their path.

The storm of bones had chewed a path through the Goreball field, reaching the gibbering mouther and sweeping it up into its growing mass. Again and again, dragon students and professors charged the tornado; again and again they were forced to fall back, the winds dispersed by the vortex rebuffing their advances. Zelli had no idea how they would take care of the problem when a dozen dragons hadn't made a dent. She licked her lips nervously, throwing glances at Bauble, wondering what the little mimic had in mind.

But she had to trust. Bauble was the smartest monster she knew but faltered with occasional cowardice. The mimic showed no such fear now, or couldn't, smashing repeatedly, now in the shape of a shovel. Zelli reached up and grabbed tight to her horns, the tearing winds of the vortex ripping at her clothing. Flash bounced from undead deer to skunk to bear, scattering each to pieces and keeping pace alongside the Danger Club.

"Throw me!" Bauble suddenly shrieked. The vortex, as if an entity all its own, veered toward them. Zelli froze. A red dragon swooped by, just avoiding the pull of the tornado, riding edge of the gale, propelled forward and toward a treant, which soon exploded in flames. The dragon bathed it in fire until the treant's head trailed red, crackling streamers.

"It's too powerful!" Zelli said, rushing ahead to stop Hugo. "Don't do it!"

"I have to! Throw me!"

Zelli gripped the owlbear's wrist. "Bauble . . ."

"Trust me, Zelli," the mimic pleaded. "Throw me, Hugo. I know what I'm doing."

Hugo hurled the shovel like a javelin toward the storm of bones. Bauble changed again before their eyes, no longer a shovel, landing on the churned Goreball field as a solid hunk of brick wall. The skeletons creating the tornado pelted into the wall, moving at such speed that the impact destroyed them immediately. Zelli couldn't make out Bauble anymore amid

the fine snow of bone powder rising from the ground. Pieces of debris shot in every direction, and Snabla raised his shield, deflecting the shards.

"The vortex has abated! Fly!" Tavian thundered.

The dragons circling nervously overhead dove down again, bypassing the tornado easily this time, targeting the treants and dismantling them with bright breathed weapons of frost, acid, and fire. The fog along the field flashed green, then red, then silvery—smoke and powdered bone obscuring everything.

A sort of stillness fell over the grounds as the tornado dissipated. Zelli looked desperately across the chaos and carnage, watching her minotaur mother bash away at a skeletal bear. Flash joined in, giving the coup de grâce for Professor Stormclash, teleporting into the bear's spinal column, snatching a bone in her jaws, and disappearing again. The undead creature crumpled, and Professor Stormclash

brought her anvil of a hoof down on the bear's broken skull.

From the base of the pulverized bone cloud came a bright red wagon wheel. It sped toward them so suddenly that Snabla shrieked, dropping down to guard against it with his shield.

"What now?" the kobold wailed.

"It's me!" Bauble's shiny eyes appeared among the spokes, and Hugo trundled over to scoop up the mimic, who once more became a shovel, ready for danger in the hands of their owlbear friend. "It worked! I can't believe it actually worked!"

"I thought you were certain!" Zelli shouted back, resting against her sword for a moment.

"Well! My calculations were careful, but there's always a chance of failure," replied Bauble, terribly cheerful.

"Or that." Tavian lifted a grass-stained claw, smoke curling from his nostrils. Through the fog of dragon breath and battle, a voice called, thin at first but gathering in strength and certitude. No words, not an incantation or spell, but a hum or drone like a swarm of insects, a million rubbing wings, a seething, evil chattering that burned Zelli's ears.

As the buzzing grew, the demolished pile of bones and bits in front of them trembled, awakening, reconstructing itself into a golem larger and thornier than

the fallen, burning, and smoldering treants littering the field. The voice of the robed figure ceased, and then, improbably, he laughed.

Beside him, another figure came into view, shambling up to the purple-robed stranger's side. It was Lord Carrion. Broken, singed manacles drooped from his wrists as he raised them and joined his compatriot in his summoning spell.

The golem jerked to life, its body the rough shape of a human, though it had no need for eyes or a mouth. Yet it saw them. Zelli shivered, feeling its knowing spread through her like a half-forgotten memory, a tip-of-the-tongue flash that quickly vanished as the ground shook, the golem came, and its ugly gray fist descended, slamming into the ground so hard that every student, professor, and standing dragon was knocked instantly off their feet.

Snabla lunged forward with his shield; Hugo raised Bauble high above his head and brought the shovel smashing down on bone-shard fingers the size of tree trunks; Zelli jabbed and hacked with her sword. The golem didn't notice a single strike.

Without warning, Tavian leapt into the air, soaring across the field toward the necromancers.

"Stop!" Zelli cried. "They're too powerful! You can't go alone!"

But Tavian was already gone, just a crimson blur as

he sped toward his doom.

Across the broken, burning, littered field, shards of bone began to float, recombining into patchwork, hideous creatures. Zelli, Hugo, Bauble, and Snabla followed the largest construct, smashing and slamming its way across the field, while other hideous creations launched into the air, careening into dragon students who had thought the day won. Zelli jumped as she ran, waving her arms, trying to draw the attention of Dean Cedaver, who glided above them on her way to follow Tavian and intercept the robed figures.

"Tavian went after the necromancers alone!" she bellowed, but Cedaver either could not or would not

hear her. The black dragon then banked sharply to the left, three reconstituted horrors diving toward her. Distracted, Cedaver recoiled and then twirled, aiming a barrage of vivid green globs of acid at the nimble, tumbling creatures.

Through the haze of blasted bone and smoke obscuring the field, Zelli watched Tavian reach the edge of the wood and the chanting, leering necromancers. The moment he came within striking distance, the stranger jabbed with his staff, knocking Tavian off course and out of the air. He pinwheeled, hitting the ground with a loud, sickening crunch.

"Keep going," Zelli told her friends. "We have to reach the other side!"

"There are too many, Zelli," Hugo called back. And he was right. There were simply too many constructs, too many new golems springing to life with each passing moment. Just holding them back and away from the school was taking its toll.

The massive golem stomping toward the academy took another step, and Zelli fought to stay upright, grabbing Hugo's shoulder for balance. Tavian had found his feet, shaking off the shock of hitting the ground with such force. Squinting, she saw him snarl and snap at the two sorcerers, and Lord Carrion turned toward him to say something. She couldn't make out the words, but Tavian roared in response.

Now the other necromancer turned his full attention on Tavian, and she froze as he collected a mass of glittering, sharp bone fragments in front of him, aiming them toward the dragon. Tavian would be skewered.

"I'm sorry, Zelli," Hugo said, seeing what she did. "We're too far . . ."

She heard Lord Carrion's vile laugh, sharp as the swipe of a blade, and then Tavian snapped off one gout of flame, catching Lord Carrion on the left side of his face. He reeled back, burned and screaming from it. The other necromancer shouted something at the dragon, and briefly they exchanged words. Zelli could only imagine what might have been said.

Without their full attention, the biggest bone construct froze, then collapsed in on itself, a plume of white smoke filling the air where it had stood.

"No give up, dragon!" Snabla shrieked, cheering with both fists in the air.

Then, swirling from above, and as if by magic, another red dragon arrived. Zelli didn't know how it had evaded the enemy, and she did not care. Its wings folded sleekly to its back, the dragon plunged toward the necromancers, taking advantage of their momentary shock. As Tavian's flames ebbed, the other dragon did not hesitate, scooping up their friend before the stranger could unleash his storm of bone fragments and retaliate.

"Zelli, look!" It was Hugo calling out to her, his taloned hand extending toward her mother and Flash.

Minotaur and blink dog were overrun. In her panic over Tavian, Zelli had failed to notice the other bone constructs continuing the fight. A dozen or so portals flashed across the grounds. Skeletal critters leapt into the glittering ovals, disappearing. Zelli clambered toward her mother and Flash, sword at the ready, the Danger Club keeping pace, but out of the corner of her eye, Zelli could see the portals flashing and closing one by one.

"Mom!" Zelli screamed, her voice raw with panic. "Mom! No!"

A grotesque bone amalgamation, part bear, part stag, and all disgusting, rammed its antlers into Flash, the little blink dog hurtling through the portal. The pup yelped, and Professor Stormclash spun to try and catch her, but stumbled into the gateway herself.

Her heart stopped and shattered, soul slashed, Zelli dropped to her knees. "Mom! That's my mother!"

Hugo, Bauble, and Snabla pressed on, and other students joined them. Patty and Gutrash fell into step beside Hugo and Snabla, hurrying toward the last place Professor Stormclash had been seen. The purple gleaming oval began to flicker, and as it did, a single hoof appeared, and then another, and then the minotaur fell to the grass, catching herself at the last moment with empty hands.

The gateway closed. Professor Stormclash crawled away from its vanishing glare, Flash the blink dog nowhere to be found.

"She'll come back," Zelli whispered, gaining her feet. She trotted weakly, then faster, finding her strength as she went to her mother, collapsing next to her and throwing her arms around the minotaur's furred neck. "Flash . . . she can teleport. She . . . She'll come back, won't she? She just has to come back. Any second now. Any second now. . . ."

Zelli tore her face away from her mother's neck, slumping onto her side. All the portals but one had faded away. Far across the field, the stranger in the purple robes dragged a burned and writhing Lord Carrion through the final gateway. They were slinking away, beaten.

The stranger's robe fluttered as he stepped through the last portal with Lord Carrion. It swallowed him up just as Dean Cedaver landed, leaving her to roar helplessly at empty air.

It wasn't over, Zelli knew, until they had Flash back, until Lord Carrion and his evil friend returned the students they had taken. Whatever victory they had won that day felt stunningly like defeat.

10

Tavian and the red dragon who had rescued him coasted down to the center of the field, where Zelli stood staring around numbly at the carnage they had only just survived.

"It isss cousssin! Cousssin Sssnarlathat!"

That, Zelli truly had not expected.

"Coussin!" Snabla threw himself at the red dragon, who coolly picked Snabla up by his tunic with two claws and placed him a respectful distance away.

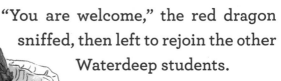

"You are welcome," the red dragon sniffed, then left to rejoin the other Waterdeep students.

"I guess he wasn't fibbing after all," Bauble said, joining Zelli and once more riding along in Hugo's shoulder bag. "Does this mean we have to take Snabla seriously?"

"Never," Zelli sighed. The wind was knocked out of her an instant later when she thought of Flash. She looked over her shoulder, willing the blink dog to pop back onto the field where the portal had been. There was nothing there but disturbed earth, scorch marks, and endless drifts of bone fragments.

Tavian trotted up to them a moment later, and Zelli felt the ground shaking behind her as other dragons gathered to meet him. His eyes darted quickly among those assembled, then landed on Zelli. He lowered his red, pointed head and pawed at the ground.

"I could not stop them," the boy dragon muttered. "I failed."

Before Zelli could assure him that he was no match for two wily necromancers, Dean Cedaver burst through their group, shoving them aside with her powerful black wings.

"Where is he? Truescale! Ah, there you are." She lifted her head high into the air, glaring down at him while more and more bodies joined their growing circle. Staff from the academy arrived, too, blinking curiously at the exchange. "What a pitiful performance. A stronger dragon would not have let those two rogues escape."

"He did his best!" Zelli shouted, forgetting that she was addressing an ancient and massive creature. Dean Cedaver turned only one eye to regard her, skewering her with a single silvery stare.

"And you are?" she sniffed.

"It isn't worth it," Tavian murmured, but he shot Zelli a grateful look. She wondered if it was the first time anyone had stood up for him.

Already, Dean Cedaver had forgotten Zelli's presence, fixing her eyes once more on Tavian. "Your utter failure aside, you could still prove useful, child. What did those miscreants say to you?"

"They said . . . They said . . ."

"Out with it!" Cedaver snapped.

And here he tossed a glance in Zelli's direction again. His voice trembled and he swallowed noisily. After a deep breath, he managed to say, "They said we have already lost, that they know where the keystone is and how to find it. Does that mean anything to you?"

Cedaver went perfectly still. Her voice, when it came, was pained. "Indeed. Indeed, it does."

"I should say so!" Dean Zxaticus had arrived, floating above the wreckage of the once flat, green, and pristine Goreball field. His ten eyestalks and single large eye were lidless and bloodshot. The remaining academy professors arrived, drifting along behind the beholder. "That defiler Carrion must have determined its whereabouts when he was loose in the academy. Catastrophic. Catastrophic!"

"Ah! And you arrive at last, Zxaticus, when all the danger has passed!" Cedaver boomed. "I might have known you would leave all the truly harrowing heroics to the dragons! Might through scholarship, that was our motto! Yet you showed not a jot of might today, only rank cowardice."

"Hey!" Zelli marched forward again, despite Tavian's murmur of warning. "Monsters fought, too, and we fought hard. If Bauble hadn't stopped that bone storm, we would have all been overrun!"

Cedaver's head cranked sharply to the side. She took Zelli's measure quickly again, then hesitated, a spark of recognition in her eyes this time. "Ah. I remember you now. And what you say is true, child. I must correct myself, Zxaticus—monsters did indeed fight valiantly, though nearly all were mere children."

"We had to protect the marker!" Zxaticus replied, breathing heavily. He closed all eleven eyeballs as if restraining himself from a complete outburst. "You

heard what that vile defiler wanted. You know why the mountain had to be protected."

"The Nexus Marker!" Bauble shouted. Zelli had never heard them use such a forceful tone. "It's somewhere in the school, isn't it? That's where the necromancers will go."

"Impossible. He will never gain entrance to the school, not when we know his plans."

"Carrion has already been inside!" Bauble squeaked, aghast. Zelli felt their frustration keenly. "Who do you think was rummaging through Zelli's things? He was looking for this Nexus thing!"

"And our protection of the grounds will increase, young mimic, without the assistance of overzealous, overconfident students."

Hugo tugged Zelli away from the squabbling deans before Bauble could turn themselves into a jack-in-the-box and launch at Zxaticus. She let him, and Bauble shifted over closer to her on Hugo's back.

"The Nexus Marker," Bauble murmured. "We have to protect it if they won't."

Zelli nodded wordlessly.

"I concur," Tavian whispered suddenly. "We must find it before those necromancers can."

Cedaver sat back on her haunches, wings folded to

her sides. The dragons had naturally coalesced behind her, the monsters gathering near Dean Zxaticus and the other academy teachers. The ebony-scaled dragon lifted her chin and twisty horns high in the air.

"The Tourney of Terror must be suspended indefinitely," Cedaver declared. The students groused and complained, but she silenced them all with a glance. "Since this disaster happened on your grounds, I think it is obvious that the Waterdeep Dragons are declared the de jure winners of the Tourney. In addition, I believe it is best that we evacuate the children. This place is no longer safe for them."

The monster students booed and jeered, but the dragons ignored them.

Zxaticus considered her proposal (and her sly bit of cheating) only briefly. "I concur, but until we can arrange for passage home, Durg, Gageth, and Ergakk will construct as many tents as possible. The children will sleep here tonight, and while our staff sweeps the mountain, all Waterdeep professors will be present to stand guard."

"It is lamentable," Cedaver sighed, surveying the ruined grounds. "But adequate." Then she turned to Tavian, beckoning him forward with one shiny claw. "And you will come with me. I want you to tell me every single word those necromancers spoke to you. Every one, do you understand?"

Tavian shot Zelli a hangdog look, shuffling away with Dean Cedaver while the dragons and monsters mingled, then dispersed. A column of smoke rose from near the bleachers again, Mavis and the fire elementals back to work, cooking up something comforting for the disoriented, frightened students. Zelli's stomach rumbled noisily, and she clamped both hands over her belly. There was no time to worry about food.

"Sssnabla ssso proud of cousssin Sssnarlathat! Brave and bessst of dragonsss!" Snabla had rushed through the crowd to find his cousin again, and sobbed against the red dragon's throat, the kobold's dirty eye mask dangling from one ear.

Slowly, Zelli, Hugo, and Bauble approached kobold and cousin.

"Well, shine my buttons and call me king," Hugo breathed. "His stories were true."

"Are you really Snabla's cousin?" asked Zelli, watching the red dragon dislodge a phlegmy Snabla from around his scaly neck. Snarlathat must have indeed made a few unwise choices, at least where enemies were concerned—his right horn was badly broken, half of it missing altogether.

"I suppose I am," Snarlathat muttered. "You must be the Danger Dummies. Snabla writes to me about you, like, all the time. Frankly, I don't see what's so impressive about you."

Bold words, considering how well the monsters had just fought, but spoken like a dragon nonetheless.

"Danger *Club*," Hugo corrected him politely with a chuckle.

Snarlathat rolled his yellow eyes. "Whatever." Before sauntering away to join the other dragons, he called, "See you around, Snabla. You owe me one."

"Yesss! Yesss!" Snabla stuck three claws into his mouth, chomping excitedly. "Sssnabla give whatever Sssnarlathat want!"

"There will sincerely be no living with him now," Bauble murmured, pages fluttering with agitation.

"It is indeed galvanizing that Snabla is related to a dragon," Hugo began, picking pieces of bone out of his feathers. "But we mustn't forget dear Flash."

"I can't believe she's gone," Zelli replied, crestfallen. "And that they almost took my mother, too! We have to find that necromancer and bring Flash home. And we have to find that keystone. Meanwhile . . ." She trailed off, staring off toward the distant shapes of Dean Cedaver and Tavian as they spoke. Just by looking at them, she could tell it wasn't going well. "Meanwhile, I have no idea what that marker even does."

"I believe I can help you with that," Bauble replied, coughing politely. "From my reading, it seems this Nexus Marker is both a key and a lock. A lock, in that it

powers the barrier protecting the mountain from certain magics, and a key in that it can turn such things on and off."

Zelli's eyes popped wide open. "The dreams . . . In the dreams Lord Carrion sent, he's trying to open something to unleash the Lord of Death he's so obsessed with!"

"A solid hypothesis," Bauble agreed. Snabla looked on, a little lost. Hugo listened quietly, talon curved under his beak. "Yes, I concur. But more than that, the barrier protecting the school inhibits teleportation magics. If that barrier falls, there is nothing stopping Lord Carrion from creating portals in and out all day long. He could abduct every student in the school!"

"Good gracious," Hugo whispered.

Zelli scrunched up her face. "Why do I feel like we're ten steps behind?"

"Because we are," the mimic replied, flipping upside down and digging through Hugo's bag. "But we can catch up. We still have Cedaver's books, remember? And now we know what the necromancers want, more or less, and where it might be. . . ." Bauble reemerged from the bag, Cedaver's books snug against them. "Like say, behind a strange, magic mirror in the caves?"

Zelli's eyes snapped open wider. "Bauble! You're brilliant!"

"*You* found the mirror, Zelli," Bauble reminded her

with a grin. "Now the Danger Club can do what it does best—"

"Hack and ssslash and basssh!" Snabla blurted, turning in a giddy circle. Clearly the encounter with Snarlathat was already speeding to his head. Zelli wondered if he would be able to effectively hide behind his shield with his ego expanding this quickly.

"No. No, Snabla! Work together! That's what we do best. *Geez.*"

"Sssnabla know! Work together!" Snabla charged on, talking right over Bauble.

The foursome gradually rejoined the Dungeon Academy students congregating near school cook Mavis's trusty cauldron. They went to the back of the line, waiting their turn for a warm bowl of something. One could not rightly study or save the school, of course, on an empty stomach. This wisdom was dispensed sagely by Snabla.

Zelli couldn't help herself. She continuously checked to see if Cedaver and Tavian were still in the clearing. She worried the dragon dean would do something rash and punish Tavian for not vanquishing the necromancers or ... or ... well, she didn't know exactly. Her exposure to dragon behavior was limited, but extreme circumstances like Dean Cedaver lunging and gobbling him up whole did enter her mind.

While they waited in line, Bauble dove headfirst, quite literally, into researching the Nexus Marker, propping one of Cedaver's hefty tomes against the back of Hugo's feathered neck while they read.

"If the keystone really is inside the school, how will we get back inside?" Zelli wondered aloud, keeping her voice sensibly quiet.

"However we can." Bauble sounded ferociously determined. "Lord Carrion might have snooped all over the school and found a way back inside, and it's only a matter of time until they think to check the caves for the key, which I am confident lies beyond the mirror Zelli found."

"The mirror," Zelli breathed. "But how will we get through it? It has some kind of curse or magical protection. We *need* a key to *get* to the key. Annoying."

"Leave that to me," Bauble replied. "I have an idea."

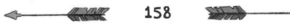

"And doesss Bauble have idea about how ssstinky Carrion essscaped?" Snabla cut in.

"Unfortunately, no," said the mimic with a weighty sigh.

"I saw him in the detention pit all chained up." Zelli shook her head, stumped. "I don't think he could have gotten free without help."

"Well!" It was Hugo's turn to heave a big sigh. "The professors will never let us in the door. Perhaps we could cultivate a very tall vine and climb into a window? Alas, no. Where would we acquire the seeds? And we would need a fast-grow potion. . . ."

"Sssneaky we mussst be," added Snabla, fixing the black sleeping mask on his head. A group of kobolds walked by, and Snabla was quick to dart in front of them, regaling them with the story of not only his chilling encounter with the necromancer in the school but Snarlathat's unexpected and timely rescue. The kobolds listened impatiently, eyeing the growing back of the lunch line.

"I can think of a solution," Bauble told them while Snabla was distracted. "But I don't think you'll like it."

"Oh great," Zelli sighed. "What is it?"

"Without Tavian, we need wings," Bauble said, eyes still moving rapidly across the pages of Dean Cedaver's book. "But we now have one new acquaintance who can fly. . . ."

Wonderful.

"Snarlathat the Unwise," Hugo and Zelli groaned in unison.

"Why do you suppose they call him the unwise?" Bauble mused.

"Maybe it's the broken horn," Zelli suggested.

"If he agrees to help, we have our answer," said Hugo.

"Got any better ideas? Ha. I didn't think so!" Bauble sniffed, not exactly giving either of them time to produce an alternative. "Who wants to tell Snabla?"

Zelli would have volunteered, but it was then that she noticed Tavian detaching himself from his conversation with Cedaver. Head hung low, he shuffled across the Goreball pitch aimlessly, seemingly in a daze. Zelli watched as Professor Stormclash intercepted him, kneeling from her great height to gently place a hand on his shoulder.

"Hugo? You do it. And save me a bowl of slop, please. There's something I need to take care of."

11

Tavian Truescale's eyes glowed gem bright at Zelli's approach. Her mother still had her hand protectively on the dragon boy's shoulder.

"This has certainly been an eventful morning," Professor Stormclash said. She sounded as weary as Zelli felt.

"I'm glad you made it out of that portal," replied Zelli. "For a moment I really thought . . . I thought . . ."

"No, dear. You're stuck with me." She winked at them both, and Zelli nodded. Later, she could tell her mother how truly relieved she felt, when they had a quiet moment in the house, warm under a crocheted blanket, the hearth blazing. It certainly had been an eventful day, and it wasn't over yet.

"How are you holding up?" Zelli asked her new friend. He was drawing looks for speaking to a monster girl. The horror. "Did Cedaver give you a thrashing?"

"That she did." He blew out a sigh, then stared back toward where the dean was rallying the dragon students. "I told her everything they said, but it's like she doesn't trust me. She says I have shown bad judgment in . . . well . . ." Trailing off, he fluttered one wing and nodded toward Zelli herself. Across the field, Professor Gast cast a low flare spell. Professor Stormclash excused herself, leaving to investigate.

"Right. You have monster stink on you now."

"Honestly? I do not feel like a dragon or a human," he muttered. "But I do feel more like myself when I'm with you and the Danger Club. You've shown me more kindness than my classmates ever have. Even your mother had only sympathy for me."

"You should eat something," Zelli pointed out, gesturing toward the line of monsters waiting to be fed. "We have a plan to retrieve the keystone. You're welcome to come along with us pathetic monsters; we could use another pair of wings."

Tavian's crooked smile told her he didn't quite believe it. "A plan? Already? And this was just another day for the Danger Club, eh?"

They made their way toward the stands. Hugo, Bauble, and Snabla had reached the front of the queue.

"I swear things aren't always so wild around here," Zelli sighed. "The other kids will give you dirty looks for being a dragon, but just ignore it. I think everyone

is too tired, afraid, and hungry to start trouble."

As predicted, every bumpy, lumpy, furry, horned head turned in their direction as they joined the rest of the Danger Club.

"How do you do this?" he asked in a careful whisper. "All the staring . . . I've always wanted nothing more than to just blend in. Will they not hate you for showing me kindness?"

"Probably, but being hated never stopped me from doing the right thing before."

Tavian laughed softly. "I have to admit, that battle today was thrilling. I've always looked like a dragon, but worried that I was just a lousy nobody. I couldn't even help my team when they needed me on the Goreball field, could never make friends . . ." He looked away, across the field, his unfocused gaze landing somewhere beyond the horizon. "In the back of my mind, I hear Morbide's voice telling me I'm nothing, but today we helped. Or, well, you and your friends did. I let the enemy get away."

"Not by choice," Zelli replied. "It isn't your fault. We'll stop them. Then the other dragons will see just how marvelous and brave you really are, and we'll have a secret laugh, knowing you've been human all along."

"Indeed," Tavian muttered, his eyes unfocused. "That is what we will do."

Hugo noticed their proximity and added a third bowl of porridge to his precarious balancing act. As soon as they were clear of the line, Zelli grabbed the food out of his arms and together they found a smooth spot on the field. Hugo took the blanket Zelli had given him out of his bag and spread it out for a picnic breakfast. When they were all seated, Zelli couldn't help but remember their first time eating together on the road to Horntree Village. They had all hunkered down around the fire, eating the stew Hugo had concocted, while Snabla ate roast meat off a spit and recounted the tale of his shield.

Bauble sat surrounded by a little fortress of open books, ignoring the hunk of goat meat Snabla had procured for them.

"Ssso," Snabla grinned, flashing sharp, tiny teeth as he stirred his porridge with hunks of goat. "Dragon musst be sssaved by Sssnarlathat, blood of Sssnabla!"

"Manners, Snabla. Not *all* dragons are arrogant monster haters," the owlbear sniffed. "Just *most*."

"I can promise I have never hunted a monster," Tavian said, placing his hand over his heart. "And I do not intend to start."

"A likely ssstory!" Snabla cried.

"Hush, Snabla, I want to hear all about your encounter with those necromancers," added Bauble reasonably. "If we are to find this keystone and protect

it, any information helps. They might have let a clue slip when taunting and threatening you!"

"Sssnabla not sssure," the kobold whispered, brooding over his bowl. "But if Sssnarlathat sssee fit to sssave you, then Sssnabla will let you ssstay. Ssstill think you have funny sssmell."

"And kobolds smell of wildflowers," Bauble murmured, receiving a sharp elbow in the spine from Snabla. "*Ouch.* Now! Snabla, contain yourself, I must concentrate. Tell me everything you can remember, Tavian."

Tavian obliged, his story somewhat unexciting. The necromancers had made the usual villainous threats, mentioning only that they were close to apprehending the keystone, and then the Lord of Death would rise to greet them all. Morning slipped away into afternoon. And while Bauble might have been listening intently, consulting Cedaver's books while Tavian told his story, Zelli noticed shifting bodies around them. An ooze drifted close, gurgling with curiosity, then a pair of air elementals glided by, treadless and silent. Then a bat-eared barghest, eyes simmering like coals. Then a harpy in a tattered housecoat. The onlookers ringed them in, creeping ever closer, tightening like an excruciating trap.

"Um, everyone?" Zelli murmured. Between an elemental and a slaad, she noted that any present

professors guarded the entrance to the school. The others must have been inside conducting the search. That meant no grown-ups were watching as a mob of monsters formed around them.

"Dragons come here, and all sorts of mischief follows," a green dretch with jagged teeth and drooping nostrils growled.

"Not a very powerful dragon, this one," a mimic spat, sidling up to the dretch, its trunk body thumping to a stop just behind Zelli, trapping her. "He chooses to hang around with these losers."

"No dragons allowed here," snarled the dretch. "Never have been, never will be!"

"Bauble!" Zelli leapt to her feet, abandoning her empty porridge bowl. "There was something I needed to show you."

The little mimic had not lifted their eyes from the books in almost an hour. "Oh?" Bauble asked distractedly. "Where?"

"Not here," Zelli bit out. "In fact, I think I should show you and Tavian. And Hugo. Why don't we all go? Snabla?"

"Indeed!" Hugo said, too loudly. "Time to go, I think!"

The owlbear fumbled to scoop Cedaver's books back into his bag, along with Bauble, who protested, then noticed their predicament and swiftly fell silent.

They all stood, but there was nowhere to go.

"Get out of my way," Zelli warned the treasure chest of a mimic that had hemmed her in. If nothing else, she felt confident she could leap over the trunk if she had to.

Tavian's hackles were up, smoke rising from between his lips and fangs. The last thing Zelli needed was their new friend roasting some idiot mimic in front of the entire school.

"No dragons allowed," the mimic echoed. "Which side are you on, minotaur?"

"Mommy minotaur won't save you," the dretch teased. The other monsters laughed, inching closer.

Zelli narrowed her eyes. "You don't scare me, *furniture*. What are you going to do, organize me to death?"

The mimic grinned, its gilded, studded lid curving upward before it opened wide, gleefully revealing six rows of stained, razor-sharp fangs.

Zelli gulped. Before she could draw her sword, Snabla stuck two claws in his mouth, warbling out the sloppiest, wettest, grossest whistle ever heard on school grounds. Then he threw his head back and roared, or at least he tried to, sounding somewhere between a sick cat and a rapidly deflating sack of wind.

"Sssnarlathat!" Snabla shrieked, punching both fists in the air. "TO ME."

The Danger Club and Tavian huddled back-to-back, squished together as the ring of monsters grew tighter and tighter. A claustrophobic itch burned along Zelli's collar. The mimic chest's tongue rolled out of their mouth, a hungry conviction shining in their eyes. A shadow flickered overhead, then spread, darkening across them until everyone—monster, human, and all those in between—looked to the sky. A red dragon descended, wings wide, the bullies scattering before being crushed to jelly.

"Two dragons are better than one!" Zelli burst out laughing, incredulous.

"Never a dull moment," she heard Tavian say.

"Snabla," Hugo said, releasing his nervous stranglehold on Bauble and his shoulder bag. "You never told us you could summon a dragon like that!"

"He can't." Snarlathat rolled his eyes, puffing a jet of steam out of his nose idly at the retreating monsters. "I heard that weird noise and had to know what was doing it. Now I know, so I'll be going. . . ."

"Wait!" Bauble almost tumbled out of the bag. "We need a favor!"

"Not interested." Snarlathat stretched his crimson leathery wings, preparing to go.

"What would it take," Bauble hurried on, "for you to fly two of us to the dormitories? Tavian can't manage all of us at once."

"Never sssplit the party!" Snabla interjected.

The dragon snorted and flicked his tail toward his kobold cousin. "What would it take? It would take this little twerp leaving me alone. No more writing fan letters. No more fawning. It's embarrassing."

Snabla's pointy trap of a mouth opened and closed a few times, then he stood quietly, chin tucked against his chest. It had to hurt. Bad. But Snabla swallowed hard and nodded, twisting his lips to the side, probably to keep from begging his cousin to take it all back.

"Sssnabla no write," the kobold managed, his chin wobbling. "Sssnabla no embarrasssment."

"Then hop on." Snarlathat flicked his head, and Snabla and Zelli crawled onto his back.

Tavian took the far larger and heavier owlbear, with Bauble in his bag. In front of Zelli, Snabla didn't seem to notice that they were lifting into the air, or that the ground was quickly vanishing. He just kept his hands close to his body and stared into empty air.

"I'm sorry, Snabla," Zelli whispered. "That couldn't have been easy. I know that dragon bloodline means

everything to you."

"Why you talk to me?" Snabla's voice wavered. "Only embarrassment."

"You're not embarrassing," Zelli assured him. "Not to me. Not to us. We're your friends, and we want you with us. Who would protect us? Who else could wield a shield the way you do?"

Little by little, the kobold's head perked up. Wind slapped against them as Snarlathat pumped his wings, taking them higher and higher. The bullies and monsters on the ground looked so insignificant from up there, just little problems that could be solved later. Zelli wanted to believe that was true, but deep down she knew, all at once, everything had changed. Flash was gone. Her mother had almost fallen through a

necromancer's portal. The school had been attacked. Even if they recovered Flash and found the Nexus Marker, she couldn't imagine going back to school and attending classes like everything was normal.

One thing at a time, she told herself. They needed Snabla to shake off Snarlathat's cruel treatment. They needed to be the bravest they had ever been—now that they were not just willfully trying to thwart two necromancers, but they were also disobeying their teachers.

Tavian and Snarlathat flew side by side in elegant tandem, close enough that Bauble could call to them above the *whoosh* of wind. "I saw the way you fought today," Bauble shouted, peering out of Hugo's pack. "The Danger Club isn't the Danger Club unless we're all together. Flash is gone, and now we need to be strong to get her back. I know you're strong, Snabla!

I've seen you walk through fire for your friends!"

Snabla's head bobbed side to side. "Do not know..."

"Well, I know." Tavian had been listening as he glided alongside a stubbornly silent Snarlathat. "Take it from a dragon: there is no doubt blood like fire runs in your veins, kobold."

Slowly, ever so slowly, Snabla raised his chin, closing his eyes against the slicing, frigid wind screaming off the mountain. "Blood like fire! Yesss. Thisss isss Sssnabla."

Zelli swiveled, carefully, and mouthed "Thank you" to the dragon boy.

Snarlathat and Tavian then pushed higher, skimming the mountain.

"There!" Hugo called over the din of the air rushing by their ears. "On the far side! Those windows!"

It was remarkable to fly! Freeing and frightening, a fast, cold, exhilarating terror that forced Zelli's stomach to flip over with each bank to the left and jerk to the right. Never in her wildest dreams had she expected to see the mountain that housed their school from this vantage. Often her life seemed to fit inside the confines of those halls and corridors and dungeons; it was easy to forget that there was a whole world outside to explore.

What were dusty paths and cobbled roads when it was possible to *fly*?

Snarlathat glided downward toward the twinkly row of windows Hugo had indicated. From a distance, the torches inside would look like no more than snow flashing gold in the sunset. Up close, however, one could make out the toys, books, candlesticks, tooth sharpeners, and statues placed along the windowsills, evidence of hundreds of monster lives and habits and tastes. The larger the student (for the academy accommodated all sorts—the needs of a small mimic like Bauble were not the same as the needs of a cyclops or owlbear) the larger the room, and therefore the larger the window. These spacious quarters were placed lowest among the dormitories, with diminishing fenestra tapering toward the mountain's peak.

It was said that a single lucky, lonely ochre jelly lived in the tallest, tiniest room.

But that was not their destination. Instead, Snarlathat and Tavian soared toward a jagged, rocky lip beside a window that would allow for Hugo's size, and that room belonged to Hugo himself. They were in sight of the window when Tavian suddenly spoke up, his voice muffled by the incessant, roaring winds.

"I hate to ruin the pleasant afternoon glide, but we're being followed."

Zelli, Hugo, and Snabla craned their necks over the sides of their mounts in unison, a small dark shape growing bigger and closer as it sped toward them.

"What is that!?" cried Zelli.

"Quickly!" Bauble had already transformed into a long, elegant spyglass. Hugo grabbed Bauble out of his bag and sent one eye down the tube.

"I believe it is . . . Shinka Bookbinder? She must have noticed us leaving the grounds. My, she is flying with alarming swiftness. . . ."

"Divert! Divert!" Bauble was suddenly fumbled in Hugo's grasp as Tavian banked to the side. The owlbear just managed to stuff Bauble safely back in his bag as the mimic finished, "You must never anger a librarian! Never! Oh but they are terrifying!"

"You know how to fly a tornado formation?" Snarlathat called to Tavian.

"Ha! The old Goreball trick? I practically invented it. . . ."

Before Zelli could ask what in the world a tornado formation was, the dragons began to twirl upward, then split apart, each taking a different route around the narrowing top of the mountain. Zelli's stomach seemed to double up on spins, and she flattened herself against Snabla's back, Snabla holding on to Snarlathat for his dear little kobold life.

"She's gaining!" she heard Hugo's distant voice, somewhere on the other side of Akhellon Ridge. Snarlathat sped back toward Tavian, the two crimson blurs meeting up and flying once more side by side.

"Flex wing," Tavian gritted out. "You make the diversion."

"What is happening?" Zelli demanded, feeling her lips flap from the intensity of the topside mountain gusts.

"You're going to jump," Snarlathat called back.

"What?!"

"Jump! Now!" Snarlathat rolled hard to the right, dislodging Snabla and Zelli without warning. They plummeted downward, but only for an instant, each of them caught in the claws of one of Tavian's strong hind legs. Zelli shrieked, Snabla cheered, and with that, his cousin began corkscrewing through the air,

back down toward Shinka Bookbinder, who pelted toward them on her tiny little black wings. Tavian flew in the other direction, making the long way around the mountain while Snarlathat made loops and blew big, angry puffs of fire.

"Don't hurt our librarian!" Bauble screamed.

"Just a diversion," Tavian assured them, keeping close to the rocky ledges of the mountain, backtracking toward Hugo's window while Snarlathat kept the little librarian busy.

Zelli thought she might be sick all over Hugo's windowpane by the time they slowed to a more pleasant glide. Just in time, too, for Tavian's legs were giving out. Zelli and Snabla tumbled against the stones, hunched there together.

"Careful, if you please," the owlbear warned as Tavian hung off the side of the mountain, waiting for his passengers to disembark. "I've grown a rather temperamental and delicate thornling on the sill, and I would hate to see it disturbed!"

"Grow a new one, Hugo; we don't have time for delicate!" Bauble groused from the owlbear's shoulders.

Snabla nimbly pulled himself up to the edge of the window, where his tiny claws hooked around the pane, scratching and searching until at last he found the hinged clasp. With a click, the clasp disengaged, and the window swung open toward them.

The kobold clambered inside, bumping the thornling and cursing as one of its needlelike appendages scraped his arm. Hugo followed, gently moving the plant aside as he wriggled his bulk into the room. The Danger Club tumbled onto the carpet, landing in a pile, Zelli knocking one horn askew. Tavian landed with a touch more grace, then turned and closed the window before they could be spotted.

"May he suffer the wrath of an angry librarian," he said quietly, perhaps only to himself, staring out the window while Snarlathat tried desperately to outrun Shinka Bookbinder, winged kobold and apparent terror of the skies.

Snabla crawled out from under the tangle of limbs, feathers, and fur. Joining Tavian at the window, he stuck his tongue out at Snarlathat and blew.

"No need ssstinky cousssin," Snabla declared, gazing up at Tavian. "Have new dragon friend now!"

"Indeed," Tavian murmured, grinning. "And you may write me as many letters as you please."

"And Tavian write back?"

The dragon boy nodded. "Tavian write back."

"Does anyone else think the school is a lot creepier this way?" Bauble hissed, riding along in Hugo's bag as they sneaked through darkened halls, pausing at each junction to listen for activity. They reached the lift down to the main corridor without incident, seeing only a single dormitory room at the end of the corridor glowing with light. From the open door came Professor Gast's rattling bone cage of a voice as he hummed to himself.

"Your school is creepy every way," Tavian replied, skulking along behind Zelli and bringing up the rear, his claws scratching lightly across the stones.

"That'sss how I like it!" Snabla's full-throated endorsement earned him a round of "shh!"s from the others. "Sssorry."

"How are we going to get to the caves without being noticed?" Zelli asked.

They had reached the lift, which was not known for being a sneaky mode of transport. The chains clanked; the gears whined; the platform itself rattled and creaked.

"The imp shafts," Bauble told them. Hugo paused beside the lift mechanism with his back to them, allowing Bauble, seated on his bag, to explain.

"The *what*?" Tavian blurted, then sighed. "I should know better than to ask at this point. Small wonder this place has imp shafts. . . ."

"Imp shafts," Bauble, impatient, raced to elaborate. "I thought I knew everything about this place until Zelli found that door in the basement! The short version? How do you think the halls and corridors get dirtied and cobwebbed? Who resets the traps? Who sharpens the wall spikes?"

Nobody ventured a guess.

"Imps, you sillies! They use a grid of narrow shafts all throughout the school to travel quickly. We can find one of their entry points and take a shaft down to the dungeon levels."

"Imps are quite small," Hugo reminded them. "Will Tavian and I even fit?"

Bauble did not appear even slightly concerned. "We will certainly find out! That way. . . ." The mimic tipped forward, indicating the path that took them past the lift and right toward the shaft of light streaming onto

the hallway carpets. Exactly where Professor Gast was conducting his search.

Just beyond that patch of light, Zelli made out a rectangular, recessed door in the wall. She must have passed it hundreds of times and never noticed. It was barely larger than a cupboard. If Hugo could fit, it was going to be awfully squeezy.

"Not a peep." Zelli placed her finger to her lips and broke away from the others, tiptoeing into the puddle of light that gleamed brighter in the hall as the sun set outside. She dared let her eyes slide to the right, peering through the wide-open door at the back of Professor Gast's floating skull. His hum continued as he inspected a student's closet. Apparently, this sweep was so thorough that they considered a necromancer could be hiding among someone's sweaters and delicates.

An orange ribbon burned above the trees outside. Black silhouettes of dragons swam through the muted yellow sky. Maybe Shinka Bookbinder was out there somewhere, putting Snarlathat through his paces.

Zelli held her breath and dug her nails into the edge of the shaft door, tugging and tugging. It wouldn't budge. She glanced at Professor Gast, who had suddenly stopped humming. Gradually, his skull began to rotate toward them. Behind her, the Danger Club and Tavian waited, frozen, hands and feet half lifted as they waited for Zelli to open the shaft.

A scarf slid free of its hook and fell in the closet, drawing Gast's attention. Saving them from detention or worse.

Zelli breathed out and yanked with both hands on the door's edge. The instant it gave, she held it open for the others, snatching Bauble from Hugo's shoulders as he passed.

"What are you doing?" Bauble whispered urgently.

"It's a sheer drop. I need you to transform."

"Into what?!"

"You'll think of something!" Gast had realized it was just a scarf on the floor. Out of the corner of her eye, Zelli could see him turning once more. "And you'll think of it now! Go!"

With a whoosh and a gasp, Zelli found herself crammed into the narrow tunnel, which plummeted

into murky, black nothingness. It might have led straight through to the other side of the world, and not just to the bottom of a dungeon. She wedged her feet against the sides of the shaft, the first in and wearing Snabla like a particularly pointy cape. Tavian hovered above them, using his wings to keep from falling, while Hugo was just visible in the shadows, clutching tight to a bright red parasol.

The shaft door shut, leaving them in deeper darkness.

"Good thinking," she whispered up to Bauble.

"Can you see the bottom?" the mimic called back, their voice echoing forever down the shaft.

"No," Zelli replied, staring through the gap in her feet. "Won't there be imps in here?"

"Not with classes out for the Tourney," said Bauble. "We can't shimmy down the whole way, it will take all night!"

"Hugo! Let go!" Zelli instructed, staring up the shaft toward the owlbear's feet. "We can all hold tight to you and glide down. Tavian will help slow us down with his wings. Let go!"

"I . . . I . . ." Hugo squawked and hugged the handle of the parasol. "I cannot! It is so far down. . . ."

"Do for Flasssh," Snabla encouraged him. "We trussst Hugo!"

"But what if there is nothing down below?" Hugo

muttered to himself. "Oh . . . I cannot. The risk is too great!"

"We're all here with you," Zelli reminded him gently. "You're the bravest owlbear we know."

"Really?" Hugo sounded genuinely surprised and delighted.

"The bravest I've met, certainly!" Tavian added.

"Well. If you all say so. Here we gooooooo—"

Hugo let go of the walls before he finished the warning, and with his weight bearing down on Tavian and Zelli, they had no choice but to do as Snabla suggested and trust. Bauble folded up, held aloft in Hugo's hand. Tavian clung to Hugo's left foot, one wing out for glide control, Zelli holding on to Hugo's right foot,

Snabla still hooked around her neck, claws digging into her throat. Away they went, faster and faster, gathering speed as they barreled down the shaft, collecting dust, cobwebs, and the occasional distracted bat as they fell.

"Ground!" Zelli shrieked. "I see ground!"

Fwoomph!

The parasol—Bauble—opened, dragging them back upward for an instant before allowing them to float gently out of the bottom of the shaft and into the familiar dankness of the academy dungeons. Zelli jumped to safety as soon as she could, Tavian opening his wings fully and gliding away when he could. Bauble closed the parasol's canopy a moment too soon, leaving Hugo to land with a thump on his bottom.

A single, mottled red imp, small and winged and horned, stared at them with unblinking yellow eyes, treading in the air a few feet from where they had landed.

The Danger Club went still. Zelli waved, bracing for the imp to shriek and alert the staff to their position. Busted.

The imp shook his head and fluttered back up toward the shaft. "I don't get paid nearly enough."

Zelli heard each and every one of them puff out a breath of deep relief.

"Snabla, we can't risk any torches right now," Zelli

said, turning to kneel and address the kobold. "Can you lead us with your darkvision?"

The kobold puffed out his chest. "Sssuperior kobold sssight, yesss! Follow, follow!"

He clasped her human hand with his far smaller one, taking her by the thumb, and they all formed a chain, Bauble once again concealing themselves as a book in Hugo's bag. Low voices rumbled from down the hall, where the spiral staircase led up to the main academy corridor. A torch flared to life. Snabla heard it, too, leading them to the slick, uneven stairs that opened like a maw into the hollows and caves below.

They had made a similar descent before, when they all pretended to be mindless thralls of the necromancer in the caves outside Horntree Village. The same pit opened up in Zelli's stomach, fluttering urgently. A premonition of terror. She stole one last glance at the dungeon level as they descended, her pulse in her throat, her hand sweating in Snabla's, her courage wavering until the kobold gave a reassuring squeeze.

Zelli looked forward and into the swallowing dark. She felt the weight of Allidora Steelstrike's badge in her pocket. Ever since the thief had been in her room, she wouldn't leave it in her drawers to be stolen. If they encountered the necromancers, her human mother would not necessarily be there to help them. This time, they would be on their own.

"Thanks to the imp shaft, we made good time," said Bauble as they reached the mysterious door deep within the subterranean caves. "We can recover the keystone and move it somewhere else before the necromancers realize it's gone."

"The dean is going to be awfully upset with us," Hugo pointed out glumly. "I know we faced a necromancer before, but we had help that time. . . ."

"Cedaver and Zxaticus are too obsessed with old grudges to see the danger before them," Tavian interjected quickly. "The weakness of the very old and very wise. Better that we take action and find the Nexus

Marker ourselves."

"We just have to be wiser." Zelli knew they were standing before the mirrored door, but only because Snabla swore it. The blackness in that pit was its own living thing, thick as treacle, entering the body on every shallow breath. "You said you figured out the way through," she added, turning toward whom she hoped was Hugo carrying Bauble. "How?"

"You'll be pleased and unsurprised to learn I puzzled that out while we ascended the mountain!" Bauble declared, smug as ever.

"While we were nearly plummeting to our deaths, you mean?" Zelli snorted.

"Exactly right! I kept returning to something Cedaver said to our dean," explained Bauble. They cleared their throat for the occasion before stoically and slowly stating: "Might through scholarship."

The words were like a key, unlocking a bright golden door that twinkled and beckoned with promise. The mirror came to life, a whole world unfolding within. But the memories it showed were gone, for it displayed the way through. It was no longer an echo of something long gone, but a very real present.

"How?" Hugo murmured, reaching out with his clawed, furry hand and finding that it passed right through the wall, into the corridor beyond the doorway.

"It sounded like a school motto," said Bauble. "When we looked into the mirror last, we saw what looked like an old academy. And when Snabla was injured, Noggin mentioned there was an age-old feud between the deans. It made me wonder— what if we weren't looking at an enchanted mirror, but a ghost from the past?"

"Bauble, I know I say it all the time, but you really are brilliant." Zelli grinned and, without another thought, stepped right through the doorway. Torches crackled to life on either side, illuminating a cavernous, stately corridor like the one high above them in the academy proper.

The others joined her, gazing around in slack-jawed

wonderment at the tapered ceilings and stained-glass mosaics on the gray stone walls. Gold-and-blue banners, faded and moth-eaten, hung like colored cobwebs from the columns placed at regular intervals down the hall. They walked in a single line together, pointing silently, dumbly, at all there was to see.

Tavian broke off from the others, wandering to a pennant hanging next to one of the mosaics. Gingerly, he lifted the torn fabric, revealing a gold-and-blue crest with an embroidered sword and filigree text. Below it, on a hammered gilt stand, rested a strong, simple golden sword.

"The Academy Blades," he read. "This was an entire school!"

Zelli joined him near the banner, then ran her hand carefully along the blade of the sword.

"It's beautiful," she whispered. Gently, Zelli drew the sword from its stand, feeling the weight of it, getting a feel for its heft and balance.

"Are you sure you should take that?" Tavian asked.

"It's not serving anyone down here, is it?" Zelli grinned and slid the blade into the belt at her side, the hilt resting against the leather strap. "Besides, I think it suits me."

"I would not want to battle someone as fierce as you with that weapon," Tavian replied.

Hugo had gone ahead and disappeared under an

archway. His voice echoed back to them, muted. "I found a classroom!"

Zelli trotted after the owlbear, sword blade tapping against her leg as she went, passing through a pale cloud of dust motes and into the room. Rows of forgotten desks sat abandoned in front of a long professor's desk and lectern. Rummaging through the desk, she discovered a framed painting. With her sleeve, she wiped the years of grime away and nearly dropped the thing.

"This is them." She stumbled over her words, thrusting the painting out for others to study. "Zxaticus and Cedaver. And look there, that's a young Impro Vice."

"Is that . . . Noggin and Needler?" Hugo hovered over her shoulder, Bauble hanging out of his pack.

"Needler looks a lot less scary," Zelli agreed. "They were friends. This was their school. . . . Dragons and monsters side by side. . . ."

"An unexpected assortment," said Hugo. He almost sounded tearful. "Just like us."

"Let's hope we have a better fate." Zelli put the frame back down on the desk and left the classroom behind.

"Come," Tavian urged them onward. "We still must find the keystone."

"It's here somewhere," Bauble assured them. "I can feel it. Listen. That low hum. Cedaver mentions it in her research, that the key and the barrier protecting the school are only possible because of an unlikely confluence of events. It's perfectly unique, one in a million. With the intersecting ley lines under the mountain and the diamonds hidden in the rocks, it creates a phenomenon unique among foci."

"In wordsss Sssnabla know," the kobold groused. He had taken one of the gold-and-blue velvet banners off the wall and swirled it around his shoulders, devoid of any historian's delicacy but looking rather dashing.

"Power," Bauble said simply. "This is a place of power."

They continued down the main, sprawling corridor. Zelli wanted to poke around in every empty classroom for hours, but she knew that would have

to wait. She couldn't believe this whole entire world lay below their school. And she couldn't believe it was such a well-kept secret. That meant the Nexus Marker must be what they theorized: something worth hiding. And if it was as powerful as Bauble said, maybe it was better left a long-buried secret.

No wonder Lord Carrion wanted it so badly. If it was this powerful and important, then maybe it might really be the key to waking up his precious Lord of Death and opening her tomb.

As they wandered, Zelli at last looked down at her feet. It was the least interesting place, but she noticed, around and ahead of them, scuff marks in the heavy blanket of dust.

"Eyes up," she murmured. "I don't think we're the first ones here."

An icy breath trickled across her neck, but when she turned to face it, nobody was there.

The ground sloped downward, the hall twisting, spiraling down even deeper into the earth. They had to be well underneath the mountain then, the air persistently chilly, an odd metallic taste permeating her mouth. Once the ground had flattened once more, and the torches before them snapped from dark to bright, Zelli saw it.

The Nexus Marker.

It was just like Bauble described—the hum, the

power, the energy emitting from it both alarming and intoxicating. A singing in her blood told her to draw nearer, but her reason screamed the opposite.

The hall became a chamber, shiny and round, as if they had stepped into the center of a white glass bead. Or a perfectly polished diamond. Shallow stone steps led to a plinth, and there sat the key of power itself. A sandstone arch waited there, carved with neat, precise runes. On an ornate stand at its center waited the Nexus Marker, a small, rectangular stone with a winking black gem at its center.

For a moment, they stood in reverent silence. They had found it: at the heart of the mountain, they had found it. They had arrived before the necromancers, and now they could plot their next move.

"It's a wonder," gasped Bauble.

"Truly it is," Tavian agreed, hurrying by them all. He ran right up to the Nexus Marker and swiped it into his grasping claws. "And as regrettable as this is to say, I must now take it for my masters."

13

"Tavian!" Zelli instinctively reached for the new yet old golden sword hanging at her side. She couldn't believe she was wielding it against a friend, but something in Tavian's golden eyes frightened her. The way he stared at the keystone . . . She shivered. "Put it back. We decide what to do with it together."

"I wish that were so," Tavian sighed, closing his claws around the keystone and backing away toward the hall that had brought them there. "I wish . . . I wish . . ."

Snabla, Bauble, and Hugo came to Zelli's side, the kobold already reaching for his shield.

"In time all your wishes might be granted, my boy," rasped a sharp, unsettling voice from behind Tavian. A voice like thousands of insects rubbing their wings. The necromancer had come, accompanied by Lord Carrion, his face horrifically burned, pink, and shiny

from Tavian's fire breath. "They will be granted by the Lord of Death, who is generous to all of her most faithful servants."

The stranger's purple robes were torn and loose, and when he lifted his skeletal hands to unfurl his hood, only bits of black scales clung to his wide-nosed skull. A dragonborn raised from the dead, alive only through dark magic.

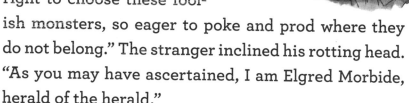

"Greetings once more, child," the necromancer said, fixing his unnatural blue gaze on Tavian as he floated to the dragon boy's left wing. "It is so good to see you again. My servant. You have outdone yourself and proved your worth. You were right to choose these foolish monsters, so eager to poke and prod where they do not belong." The stranger inclined his rotting head. "As you may have ascertained, I am Elgred Morbide, herald of the herald."

"You betrayed us," Zelli hissed, eyes flying to Tavian's. "How could you? I thought we were friends! I thought we were—"

"The same?" Morbide gave a harsh cackle and flicked the amulet off Tavian's neck. At once, the

charm was broken, and Tavian, a human boy, crumpled to the floor.

"Sssnabla knew! Sssnabla sssmell this deceit!" the kobold shouted, jabbing toward them with his shield.

"Do not underestimate them," Lord Carrion warned. "They are crafty little imps."

"Your failure is a conversation for another time, Carrion. It is perhaps fitting that the boy's ruse was performed so . . . enthusiastically. Those burns are a trifle compared to the punishments I could devise," said Morbide. Tavian lunged for the amulet, but the necromancer easily kept it out of reach, floating away. "Now, now, boy, do not be greedy. Hand me the Nexus Marker."

"Don't listen, Tavian," Zelli warned. "You don't have to listen to him!"

The sandy-headed boy slumped, and curled his hands into fists. Shaking, he pursed his lips together. "But I do. I must listen to him. He has been my teacher and mentor all my life; he gave me the red dragon amulet so that I might become strong."

"And without it you are pitiful," Lord Carrion reminded the boy, his face now resembling melted and re-formed pink wax. Not without some satisfaction, Zelli noticed a number of bruised welts rising on his hands and face. The spiders. "With it, you are cunning, vicious, and a great and believed deceiver! Look

how easily you tricked these meddlesome children!"

"Not trick Sssnabla," the kobold insisted on pointing out.

"How did you even get inside the mountain?" Zelli asked. She was stalling for time, hoping Bauble or Hugo might formulate a sudden plan to save them. "The magic here protects against teleportation."

"We simply followed you, child. Thank you kindly for the imaginative entrance." Morbide grinned, showing crooked fangs. "Your friend had already distracted any airborne defenses, and assembling a winged creature is no challenge for a necromancer of my skill. The chute down to the dungeons was not the most *dignified* means of conveyance, but it served. It served."

It was then that she noticed the dust and cobwebs clinging to the necromancer's already dirtied robe. They had all but cleared a path for these two menaces to follow. Zelli's palm itched to swing the golden sword. Her eyes slid to Snabla and then Hugo, but nobody seemed willing to make the first move.

"All this over a stupid key?" Zelli spat. They were trapped with no way out behind them, their enemies guarding the only corridor back to the school.

"Our portals are powerful; they can travel to any place, and any plane, yet they cannot be used inside the barrier of Akhellon Ridge. The Nexus Marker not only

nullifies that barrier, it nullifies that which keeps our most dreadful master trapped," the lich purred. "Once the keystone is ours, the Lord of Death will rise."

"I told you, girl," Carrion giggled. "I told you!"

"Tavian!" Elgred barked. "The marker! Now!"

The boy stared down at the keystone in his hand, then he looked to Zelli. "I am sorry."

He handed the keystone to Morbide, a visible shudder passing through the necromancer lich's body as he finally held it in his decayed hand.

"And so everything you said, Tavian, everything you told me . . . it was a lie. It was all a lie!" Zelli gripped the sword harder. Her heart raced, a sick feeling making her want to scream, cry, and vomit all at once. She had never felt betrayal like this before. "We were kind to you. We accepted you!"

"You were our friend," Hugo added softly.

Morbide flung the amulet on the ground at Tavian's feet. It cracked, one lovely golden link skittering across the floor.

"There is your prize, boy," Morbide muttered.

"But the Lord of D-Death," Tavian stammered, scrambling to retrieve the amulet. Rather than making Zelli angry, it only made her feel sad. All this so he could pretend to be a dragon? All this, and he didn't get to have a family or friends? His must have been a terrible and lonely life, to make Morbide his best chance for happiness. "You said she would make me a prince. You said she would give me power!"

Morbide rolled his bulging, exposed eyes, opening his hand and flattening his palm, a spell sparking to life, a miniature tower made of sand rising from his fingertips. "Far to the east, beyond these lands, within a maze of dunes, at the end of a starless desert, lies a forgotten kingdom beneath Anauroch. It and its master slumber, but soon they will know life. Our forces gather there, but they hunger. Oh, how they hunger for fresh meat." The tower collapsed, shifting into a pile of sandy bones. "The desert has yielded unto us and coughed up a riches of bones, but we need more. And when we are fed, when we rise, when we know our full power, we will rival even the Netherese. There is no life there left for us to take, and so your land will swell our undead armies and feed our hungering master. The Lord of Death, the Herald of Teeth and Eyes."

Well, I hate that, thought Zelli, taking a step forward with her sword brandished.

"A valiant gesture, but an empty one," the lich sighed, a glowing, bluish-silver chain extending from his left hand and capturing her wrist. It burned like icy fire, and Zelli cried out, dropping her sword. It clattered uselessly down the step.

"I would destroy you myself," Morbide continued, his hideous dragon skull smiling. "But I will leave that pleasure to my better. Her hunger will be twice sated by those who struggle so exquisitely and cling with hopeless tenacity to life."

"Where isss Flasssh?" Snabla shouted, his shield knocked out of his grasp by another icy chain before he could even try to swing it. "Where isss our friend?"

"I know not the answer," Morbide replied, bored. "But if she happened through my portals, then she, too, will soon feed my master."

"Likely she is already dead!" Carrion added, then grew silent when Morbide gave a sharp look.

"Master this and master that! Who is it? We defeated you once before, and we can do it again!" It was Bauble's turn to speak up from Hugo's bag. Zelli's wrist was in agony, and the more she twisted against the chain spell, the more it hurt. If Tavian felt sure they could overcome Morbide, he did not outwardly show it. He still knelt on the ground, shaking, clutching the cracked amulet.

"Little trifle," the lich said, almost fondly. "Your

mind would turn to dust before you even perceived my master." A dozen frozen chains leapt from the lich's hands, snatching hands, wrists, ankles, and necks, binding them all to the palm of his hand.

Binding Tavian, too.

"You promised!" Tavian cried, the amulet swinging by a single loop from his pinkie finger. "You promised I would be a prince. . . . I served you my whole life. I never wavered. I was loyal!"

"You were a pawn," the lich shot back.

Elgred Morbide crushed the sand in his hand. When he lifted it again, an entire mirage burst from his palm.

"Behold," he stammered, enthralled by his own creation. Lord Carrion sucked down a wheezing gasp of ecstasy. "An'Kizhek, Azure Dracolich, She of Unending Hunger. Mother of Nightwalkers, Empress of the Lost Sands."

"Dracolich?" she heard Bauble choke out. "Oh no."

Zelli did not need to know what nightwalkers or dracoliches were to decide they were in deep trouble. There stood a towering creature, once a dragon but now a horror of jagged bones and leathery flesh. Blue, lightning-like enery seethed where her innards should have been, a white spike of a horn rising from her skull like a giant's sword. Beneath her stirred an army of tall, shadowy creatures, spindly thin. Their eyes

glowed with the same indigo flames as the dragon's belly. An'Kizhek somehow *saw* her, though it was only the lich's conjuration. As soon as those eyes found her, Zelli felt her soul shudder with regret, as if somehow her body felt embittered toward its own spark of life.

"Ah," Morbide whispered. "Is she not impossibly, perfectly arresting?"

He did not wait for an answer, which would inevitably be: "No" or "Under no circumstances" or "Do you have eyes?" etc., but instead he glided toward Tavian, gently patting him on the head while he lifted the Nexus Marker high into the air.

"I will enjoy feeding you to my master most of all," he told the boy.

Zelli had just enough freedom to twist around and watch in horror as the lich ran his bone nub of a thumb over the black gem on the keystone. With her free hand, Zelli went searching in her pockets. It was hopeless, she knew, but she had to try. She found Allidora Steelstrike's silver cloak badge in her pocket and held tight. Closing her eyes, she whispered the words Allidora had made her memorize.

"By sword and by light, Talos guide my sight, summon my kin, call the Steelstrike. By sword and by light, Talos guide my sight, summon my kin, call the Steelstrike. . . ."

Nothing happened and then, with a stomach-

clenching pulse, everything happened. Lord Carrion screamed in excitement; Tavian groaned, shielding his eyes. Morbide activated the keystone, a pale light rippling out from the Nexus Marker, a deep boom echoing throughout the core of the mountain.

"We have to stop him," Zelli heard Bauble whisper desperately from inside Hugo's bag. She agreed, but how? Her birth mother's amulet had done nothing, and now Morbide had the one thing he and Lord Carrion had craved more than anything. They had used Tavian to get it, and betrayed him, too, in the end.

"Tavian," Zelli murmured, trying to get his attention. Lord Carrion and Morbide were too busy bathing in the glory of their victory to notice her shooting dagger eyes at the boy. At last, he raised his head, the amulet still balanced on one finger.

"I'm sorry."

"Don't be sorry," Zelli replied. "Be our friend." She looked intently at the necklace. Broken or otherwise, it might still turn him into a dragon. Their odds against the necromancers were much, much better with a dragon on their side. She tried to understand. She tried to think of who she might have become if her mothers had not loved her and accepted her. Tavian had done the wrong thing, but she couldn't say if he had ever really been shown the right thing, or been given the space and safety to risk a bit of genuine

bravery. Zelli looked at Carrion's burned face—Tavian had fought back, even if accidentally. Maybe he wasn't so far gone; maybe he didn't want to betray them and that puff of fire breathed against Carrion's face had been the beginning of a whole new hero.

Sometimes it just took one small rebellious step. . . . The first step was hard, but all the ones after it came easier.

"Use the amulet," she whispered fiercely. "Help us! Fight back with us!"

Tavian bit down hard on his lip, staring at the amulet as if it might grow teeth and snap at him. "I don't . . . I don't want to be that dragon anymore. I can't be a red dragon again."

"What are you doing, girl? Be silent!" Morbide's milky eyes grew wider as he twisted the icy chains holding Zelli's hands. She cried out in pain, but fought the urge to obey him. Morbide dragged her down to her knees, but she didn't give up.

"Then be something else!"

Out of the corner of her eye, she saw Hugo and Snabla nodding along with her words.

"I can't," Tavian choked out. "It's a red dragon amulet!"

"Yet all your life this fiend lied to you," Hugo reminded him. "He filled your head with nothing but empty promises. . . ."

Tavian didn't seem to hear them, lost in his contemplation of the amulet that had been the source of his power but now no longer seemed to hold any temptation. As he beheld the necklace, strange colors danced along his skin, a flickering like shadows, shadows of scales. They were red one instant, then green, and then brown. Zelli glanced over at Hugo, who also seemed to be observing the strange phenomenon on Tavian's skin. Zelli glanced over at Hugo, shrugging helplessly.

"Statue of Cyric!" Hugo blurted.

"I said *silence!*" Morbide yanked on the chains holding Hugo, sending the owlbear sliding across the platform.

"Statue of Cyric," Hugo wheezed, breathing shallowly on his side.

It sounded like gibberish to her at first, and she could not believe Hugo was wasting precious time, but then she remembered the two boys chatting away about one of their shared loves, Goreball. And clearly it meant something to Tavian. His eyes snapped open, sun bright, and he gripped the amulet harder, then ducked his head, sliding the necklace on with his mouth in a grim line of determination.

"What foolishness is this?" Morbide groaned, whirling toward Tavian.

Before their eyes, Tavian transformed, a spray of

fresh seawater splashing all of them as a bright light flashed where the human boy had been.

"I am not a red dragon" came Tavian's voice, strong and sure. "I am not greedy; I am not evil...." The spray subsided, revealing a sleek bronze form, a dragon with shimmering wings, tipped with iridescent green. Four large horns protruded from the side of his head, with smaller points running along his chin and jaw. Morbide's chains still held him, but the dragon looked completely unbothered by it. "I am Tavian Truescale, clever and just, a bronze dragon by choice and sworn enemy of Elgred Morbide and the Lord of Death."

14

There he is at last, thought Zelli. *Our friend.*

"The amulet!" Lord Carrion screamed, hurrying to Morbide's side. The lich still held the keystone aloft, his other hand puppeteering the frozen strands of magic holding the Danger Club and Tavian captive. "He knows, Morbide! He knows!"

"It matters not," Morbide said, though his nose wrinkled with agitation. "The keystone is activated. We can no longer be sto—"

Before the lich could finish his thought, Tavian drew in a quick, sharp breath, sending a hard jolt of lightning across the room, his roar a terrible blast. Lord Carrion shot past Zelli, a whining purple blur as

he slammed into the opposite side of the chamber and collapsed in a grunting heap. Morbide's milky, slitted eyes flared wide as he beheld his fallen compatriot. At once, he summoned a portal, one that would now carry him far from the school with the barrier nullified.

"Farewell, Truescale. We will meet next as enemies, and I will not tell the Lord of Death to show you mercy," spat the lich. "You will beg to be my servant once more before you meet your doom."

"Never!" Tavian shouted, the fins on his dragon neck fluttering.

"Never is such a very long time," Morbide chuckled. "And the lady of all our ends comes with haste."

Then he was gone, floating toward the portal, arms outstretched as if to receive the embrace of a loving parent. Abandoning Tavian. Abandoning Carrion. Zelli watched, powerless to stop him. Tavian drew in another breath as if to topple Morbide, too, but the lich cast one more spell, a final icy chain shooting from his hand and wrapping around Tavian's long nose, locking it shut.

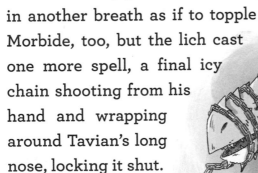

"Bauble . . . ," she heard Hugo

mutter as he lay on the floor. The bag on Hugo's shoulders was moving, rustling. . . . "Bauble, what are you doing?"

"He can't win. I won't let him. He uses knowledge for awful undead evil, and I won't let him get away with it!" The mimic took a page out of Morbide's own book, growing links, lengthening into a chain, a manacle just like the one locked around Zelli's wrist closing instead around the lich's thin, bony ankle.

"Bauble! No!" Zelli heard the words leave her mouth, saw the portal undulate and receive Morbide, and watched as the mimic chain clasped around his leg whipped free of Hugo's bag, magic chain secured to living chain.

Before Bauble was gone, she saw their eyes open on the manacle and seek her out. One instant of recognition, and then, along with the lich, Bauble was gone.

In a daze, Zelli heard the professors arrive. Their voices reached her across deep water, across a void, tugging her back from the numb paralysis she had slipped into the moment Bauble had gone through the portal without them.

Follow, a whisper inside her said. *Go after them.*

But Hugo had seemed to hear that voice inside her and joined her near the lich's portal. His big, furry hands clamped down on her shoulders, keeping her

from doing the unthinkable. The lich's chains no longer bound them. A vivid purple bruise pulsed on Zelli's wrist.

But Bauble had thought it. Bauble who was nervous and bookish and couldn't turn into anything more threatening than a dustpan. She or Snabla should have been the ones to do something reckless, but no . . . Bauble had gone through. Bauble was gone. And then, an instant later, before Zelli could make up her mind, Morbide's portal disappeared.

"The worst has happened," she heard Zxaticus say behind her. "The Nexus Marker taken, the mountain's barrier destroyed."

"No, it's worse than that!" Her rage gave her renewed life. Zelli leapt to her feet, pushing Hugo away and storming up to the beholder floating just at the edge of the stairs leading up to the arch that had held the keystone. "My friend tried to stop the dragonborn lich Morbide, and now they're gone! They're . . . They did more than you ever did! You're cowards! You're all cowards!"

In the diamond rotunda the word *cowards* lingered for an agonizing eternity.

The beholder bobbed up and down, holding his tongue, his biggest eye half-lidded with sadness.

"Morbide." She heard Cedaver, who had also come, gasp. The room was getting crowded—Noggin

and Needler, Impro Vice (transformed into a small, wheeled cart), Professor Gast and Professor Cantrip had all come. Late. They had come *late*.

"This is our doing," Zxaticus murmured. "What you see here—this old school, this gateway, these faded memories—it is all our doing."

"We were once educated here in harmony," Cedaver explained. She was again transformed to fit inside halls fit for monsters and not dragons. Striding forward, she gazed beyond them, staring at where the keystone had waited. She spoke through a tight jaw. "Inseparable, really. That was us. But when we were older and it came time to oversee the school together, Zxaticus and I could not agree on anything."

"I despised her most trusted advisor," said the beholder. He paused for a suspiciously long time. "Elgred Morbide. He thought monsters were below him, below anyone with draconic blood. Our differences grew too contentious, too bitter. We decided to hide the Nexus Marker forever, and the old school with it. Buried, we thought, it would not be a threat."

Cedaver drew her wings back, her face so tight Zelli thought it might shatter. "We charged the monsters with safeguarding this hidden relic. It was not long after I established the Waterdeep School for Dragons that Morbide became . . . odd. Unruly and reclusive. I soon learned he was conducting unsanctioned

experiments in my school, tampering with undead magics that I could not abide."

Tavian came forward slowly, almost skulking, nervous to be seen in this new bronze form. "And you banished him, I suppose. And he went off to conduct his experiments elsewhere. He took me from my parents, made me his servant, and gave me this amulet, telling me I could only serve by finding the keystone. The dragons did not possess it, so I had to persevere, and wait, and bide my time until I could search here, too. I was never allowed to rest, or stop, or think of anything but his commands."

The ebony dragon balked, then her eyebrow ridges knit together with concern. "You have . . . changed. This is the amulet's doing?"

"I'm . . ." Tavian hesitated, but Zelli gave him a single nod. It was his decision. He got to decide his own story, his own identity. "I'm a bronze dragon; that's what is truly in my heart. Morbide had me fooled, but now I know what I am. I betrayed you, and the school, and my new friends, but that will never happen again."

Cedaver drew up her shoulders and approached the boy, carefully, oh so carefully, laying a single hooked claw over his shining bronze scaled shoulder. "The others will reject you. A bronze dragon is not welcome among us. The rift between the metallic and chromatic dragons is ancient and immovable. They would want you hurt, punished, but I sense you have been punished enough."

Tavian met her eye, standing tall. "From now on I will find my own way, carve my own path. I think first I need to consult with my friends."

"Friends?" Cedaver frowned, then noticed who he was addressing: the Danger Club. "I see."

"You really don't," growled Zelli. "We managed to set our differences aside and we're kids! What's your excuse? This petty grudge put us all in danger, and now Morbide is waking up a dracolich and nightwalkers in the desert! Without the barrier to protect us, he can teleport here and feed us all to his new friend for a midnight snack!"

Zxaticus and Cedaver fell silent. At last, the beholder floated toward her, solemn and subdued. "This has given us much to discuss. It seems it is time for Dean Cedaver and me to reexamine the relationship between our great institutions. If Morbide has truly located a dracolich, then we will not stand a chance against them unless we are united. This threat

cannot be ignored, but it may take more than the might of the Dungeon Academy and the Waterdeep Dragons to quell it."

Zelli couldn't help herself. "I'm going to hold you to that," she blurted. But she wasn't alone. Hugo and Snabla went to stand beside her, then, to her surprise, Tavian did, too. Bauble was . . . Zelli couldn't think about it. It was too much. Too hard. She went slowly down the stairs, away from the arch. Taking the golden sword in hand, she lifted it to her chest. "Morbide and his followers have attacked students from our school twice. There won't be a third time if the Danger Club has anything to say about it."

"What do we do about him?" Hugo asked, pointing to the clump of burned flesh, spider bites, and torn robes in the corner.

Lord Carrion.

"I have a sssign for him," Snabla muttered, rubbing his paws together.

Lord Carrion snored on, completely—and perhaps fortunately—oblivious to his predicament.

Epilogue

Zelli ran her hand across the Steelstrike badge resting on top of a red-and-gold crocheted blanket. Two reminders of home. She would need them both, she thought, to go confidently down the path she had chosen.

Or maybe not.

She glared at the Steelstrike badge, wondering what exactly it was for if it didn't work when she needed it most. Had she not used it correctly? At her lowest, at her most powerless, she had said the words her birth mother had told her, but nobody appeared to assist. Maybe the spell on it was broken, or maybe Allidora Steelstrike had already moved on.

Hugo sat on the floor beside Zelli's bed in her dormitory. He had brought her a little plant to brighten her room, and it sat in his lap, leaves actively reaching toward the wan light dribbling in through the window.

Snabla stood at the sill, watching drag-ons tumble through the sky in the distance. Try as he might, he couldn't entirely shake his love for the flying creatures. He bounced up and down when-ever a dragon corkscrewed nearer to the mountain.

Zelli. Hugo. Snabla.

Three. *Three.* Their numbers had been slashed from five to three. Were they even the Danger Club without Bauble? How would they go on without their brilliant friend? Zelli swallowed a horrible lump in her throat. Days had passed, but the sting of losing Flash and Bauble remained fresh. They would probably lose even more if they went through the portal after their comrades, but how could they sit by and do nothing? Bauble had been so surprised when Zelli expressed an interest in research and knowledge, but it had felt right to Zelli at the time. Paths diverged. Roads some-times had detours. In the end, Bauble had changed, too, the bold, fearless one following the necromancer lich to a terrible unknown.

They had all made their choices, but where would they lead?

A knock at the door startled her.

Tavian Truescale had come, green and bronze scales as bright as polished treasure. As bright as the golden sword Zelli intended to bring on their journey.

"Am I intruding?"

"Truessscale!" Snabla called, gesturing him inside. "Friend!"

"Friend," Tavian repeated, trying out the word. "I feel I do not yet deserve such kindness." He took a few steps into the room, hesitating on the rug near her roommate Bloppy's empty, made bed. "You showed me true goodness, and I repaid you with lies."

"He raised you, Tavian; you didn't have a fighting chance," Zelli told him, turning and sitting on the edge of her mattress. "I got lucky with who found me, who loved me, and it took me a long time to find my friends. It changed me, just like it changed you." She nodded toward his new and more fitting form.

"But how did you know I could change?" asked Tavian.

Hugo grinned shyly. "I saw your scales flickering and changing colors as you held the amulet, and I thought: Maybe, just maybe, he can overpower the magic in the necklace and become something else."

Hugo ventured a guess, saying, "It could be an Amulet of True Draconic Polymorph. I've heard of such charms, but they're incredibly rare!"

"Morbide would never have let me take the amulet if I knew it was capable of this," Tavian added. "He wanted me to believe I was his pawn, and telling me I could only take one form was just another of his hundred lies."

"Now you sssmell right," Snabla agreed. "Sss-till, Sssnabla keep one eye on you. Very wide eye. Alwaysss."

"Fair," Tavian murmured.

"Statue of Cyric," said Hugo, gently running a claw over one leaf of the plant he had brought. "We share a common interest."

"Goreball plays," Tavian chuckled, though still he seemed hesitant. "An unexpected hand of friendship in my darkest moment."

"But you took that hand," Hugo told him. "You took it when it mattered most."

"So *that's* what that means," Zelli cried, rolling her eyes. "Statue of Cyric. I never thought Goreball would save our skins."

"It certainly flew right over Morbide's head," the dragon added, venturing another step toward them.

"We don't know him like you do. But we will," said Zelli. She nodded subtly to the half-empty bag beside her.

"Oh?" Tavian asked.

Hugo stood, placing the plant on the sill near Snabla. A dragon soared by, cerulean blue. It roared, unleashing a cloud that sprinkled real snow down the mountainside.

"I'm packing my things. We're preparing for a journey." Zelli crossed her arms over her chest and

addressed them all, fiercely determined. "We're going to the dunes, to the starless desert. We're going to find Morbide and this master of his, and we're going to bring Flash and Bauble home."

Hugo went to her side, adjusting his woolly vest with a nervous chuckle. Snabla launched onto the bed, fists on his hips as he waited for Tavian's response.

"So." The dragon boy grinned. "When do we leave for Anauroch?"

That was the spirit, thought Zelli. The Danger Club spirit.

DUNGEONS & DRAGONS®

Dungeons & Dragons: Dungeon Academy: Tourney of Terror
Wizards of the Coast, Dungeons & Dragons, D&D, their respective
logos, and the dragon ampersand are registered trademarks
of Wizards of the Coast LLC in the U.S.A. and other countries.
© 2022 Wizards of the Coast LLC. All rights reserved.

Manufactured in Italy.
No part of this book may be used or reproduced in any manner
whatsoever without written permission except in the case of
brief quotations embodied in critical articles and reviews. For
information address HarperCollins Children's Books, a division of
HarperCollins Publishers, 195 Broadway, New York, NY 10007.

www.harpercollinschildrens.com

ISBN 978-0-06-303914-8

Book design by Elaine Lopez-Levine

22 23 24 25 26 RTLO 10 9 8 7 6 5 4 3 2 1
❖
First Edition

Professor Zxaticus

Noggin and Needler